sim ·u ·la ·crum

[sim-*yuh*-**ley**-kr*uh* m]

noun

1. a slight, unreal or superficial likeness or semblance

2. an effigy, image or representation

my Lord

The ROTHVALE LEGACY

II

RAINE MILLER

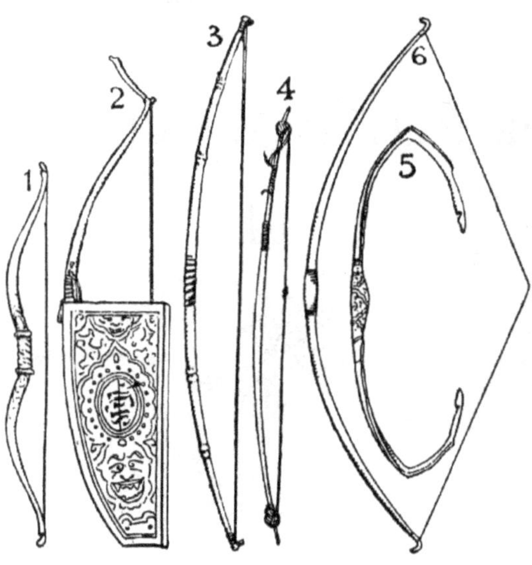

my Lord

The ROTHVALE LEGACY
II

Copyright © 2021 *Raine Miller Romance*
All rights reserved.
Cover by *Jena Brignola.*
Proofreading by *Proofing With Style.*
Editing by *CC Readings.*

DEDICATION

For Dora

*I remember my mother's prayers and they have always followed me.
They have clung to me all my life.*

—ABRAHAM LINCOLN

AUTHOR'S NOTE

I BEGAN WRITING THIS STORY IN 2011. It was envisioned and outlined before I ever penned **Naked**. Yes, it's true. I have my composition book with the original notes to prove it. It's all there in black and white. I treasure that simple book with the handwritten ideas and scribblings about a reluctant Lord of the Realm and a stubborn art conservationist. Of course, it all got put on hold when I found my inspiration for Ethan Blackstone and Brynne Bennett's story in the Blackstone Affair... but I never forgot about my original characters of Gaby and Ivan. In fact, I placed them smack dab in the middle of my Blackstone world on purpose so I <u>couldn't</u> forget about them. I wrote their beginnings into the climax at the end of **All In** so that I'd be forced to tell their story at some point.

Priceless was published six years ago now. It very much pains me to type that number since it was left in a cliffhanger. (I ***do*** have a heart in case you were wondering.) If you're reading this, I want to reach out and thank you from the bottom of my heart for sticking with me for those six long years. *I want you to feel my crushing, too-long hug and the sloppy kiss to your cheek right now through whatever device you're reading these words on.* Truly. I don't even have the words to express my thanks and gratitude for holding on for all that time just to have the chance to read more about my kinky British Lord and his feisty, but wounded Lady as they find their true soulmate in each other.

I assure you they are precisely where you left them six years ago. Like one second for each year you've had to wait. So six seconds of time have passed since you last saw them in bed together "talking" about what Ivan would like to have from Gabrielle.

I so love the ability to do magic like that as an author.

It's a joy for me to be bringing the next part of their love story to you now. Theirs is a very big, romantic story. So much more complex than I ever imagined it when I first started it back in 2011. But then an idea comes along and takes on a life of its own and I have to just let the story take me where it wants to go, surprising even me as I'm writing it. Ivan and Gabrielle's tale is one of those.

It's been a delight to be back in their romantic, kinky, sexy world for sure. I hope you feel the same way.

xxoo R

Prologue

1st May 1862
London

Dearest Augusta,

    I hope my letter finds you, my dear, loving niece, in good health and all is well within your family. I am writing to share with you an experience of great inspiration and enlightenment for me. Last month I was pressed upon by my friend Mr. Victor Rampling to accompany him to a dinner party in Warwickshire at a grand estate, hosted by none other than Sir Tristan Mallerton. As you know he is nearing the twilight of his life, but I was graced with his companionship and counsel for the course of a whole evening, which was remarkable in itself, but what I saw and learned that night within his company, so inspired and marked upon my spirit that I shall remember it to the very end of my life.

Gavandon, Warwickshire is the country home of Lord Rothvale IX, who if you might recall, is a founding member of the National Gallery we talked about before, a greatly respected politician in the upper house, and also a patron of the arts in word and deed. He has gifted many personal works to the Gallery over the years since its founding in the year of our lord, eighteen and twenty-four.

The Rothvales have since retired to their country estate in Ireland at Belfast. It is not expected that they shall ever live permanently in England again, preferring instead to live out their remaining days in peace and tranquility in that country, in reflection of a long and productive life as a public servant to the crown. Sir Tristan Mallerton is long associated with the Rothvales, being as close as any family member of blood would be, having lived with or near to them for most of his life. He was charged with the closure of their estate at Warwickshire and was in the process of preparing to move some works of art from Gavandon House for shipment to the Rothvales in Ireland. One painting he showed to me held great personal sentimentality to Lord and Lady Rothvale, who were so beloved of the work individually, which spoke to their desire to have it for the walls of their home in Ireland rather than left behind in Warwickshire.

Augusta, I must describe for you this magical work of purest art and beauty—a priceless treasure that I cannot ever forget from my memories, no matter how long my life may be. It appears in my dreams still and calls to me all the time that I must paint my own version from this exquisite creation of colors and canvas. I will not do it now, of course, while Sir Tristan is still a living artist of legend. Having no wish to disrespect his great vision, I will wait until an appropriate time for presenting my simulacre of his resplendent conception to the world.

I have made many notes and some sketches though, so I may not forget a single detail of the otherworldly beauty which I was blessed to witness that night. The work is of a woman sleeping in a chair wearing a splendid yellow gown. Her feet are tucked up underneath her as she sleeps, her faithful dog at her feet, and also her writing desk and pen and journal. She has the most extraordinary Indian shawl of a gold and orange threaded design wrapped about her, and her golden hair is loose upon her shoulders as if she floats upon a lake. It is ethereal in its presentation of the beautiful subject reminiscent of a goddess at her slumber, dreaming of things only a goddess would dream. Sir Tristan shared with me that the subject is none other than Lady Rothvale herself, painted shortly after her marriage to Lord Rothvale in the year of our lord, eighteen and twelve, more than fifty years ago. His love for her is there in the paint, Augusta. It is as clear to see even if the person who looked at it were nearly blind already. Sir Tristan told me he painted her in June on a summer's day when her husband happened upon her by chance and decided he would like to have it as a portrait of his beloved bride. A boy was sent with a message to bring Sir Tristan immediately to the house where he set about taking over from Lord Rothvale's preliminary sketching onto a canvas where the initial shape and form of her was put down already by his hand. Lord Rothvale discovered her asleep in her pose and then had the forethought to have Sir Tristan set it on canvas in his masterful hand. Sir Tristan told me that he never even spoke to his friend about what he was to do on the day. It was an unworded understanding between the two men. He simply entered the solarium where Lady Rothvale was sleeping and knew exactly what he was being tasked to do. They also had no wish to awaken her, so they remained silent as they worked at a furious pace. Sir Tristan told me Lady Rothvale slept on for such time as the two of them were able to get enough of her form drawn that first day to finish the portrait from later sittings he arranged with her.

He called his painting, "Sleeping Imogene" when he presented it to me, and I could sense his deep attachment to this singular work as a very special one to the great man himself. Lady Rothvale is called Imogene by her Christian name. He said it with such affection and remembrance of love it was apparent to me, even in my novice days as an artist, of the deep friendship and bond of love between them.

It was truly "something of the marvelous" my darling, to quote the words of another, Aristotle, I believe. I only wish you could have seen it with your own eyes. I know you would have appreciated the beauty and magic the portrait evokes upon the eye and within the heart.

I look forward to seeing you in the autumn and viewing your own work and hopefully to collaborate on a project as we artists must do, just as we must continue taking our next breath. Be well, my dearest.

Your most loving uncle,

Frederic

Chapter 1

25th August
Donadea, Northern Ireland

My heart dropped as I froze against Ivan. He sensed me stiffening and held on to me a little tighter. Unable to move away or do anything much more than just stare at him, I memorized every feature of his face, the gorgeous green eyes; the mole on his upper left cheek, the natural part of his hair and the way it fell along the side of his face, the color of his lips and the shape of his jaw. All parts of him I was just beginning to know by heart.

All of him beautiful to me, to the point I almost couldn't look away.

His burning gaze held me anyway, just as much as his arms were doing. Ivan held on to me because he expected me to run away and freak out. He was only reacting to what he'd come to expect from me based on his experience. I'd been trying to run from him nearly every time we'd been in the same space together since our very first meeting. His powers of deduction didn't have to work overtime to figure me out. He also had no trouble trying to convince me to stay with him longer. Ivan Everley was a master of persuasion.

I want you submissive when we fuck, Gabrielle.

I shivered at the thought... and the implications of what he meant by those very direct and potent words. Imagery flickered through my brain and threatened to short it out. This man had a powerfully mysterious hold over me that I'd never experienced before, and I needed to exercise extreme caution. My rational mind knew this, of course, but I also knew I was in danger of tossing said extreme caution to the proverbial wind.

The confidence with which he made his

request inferred this thing we'd started would be continuing indefinitely. As much as it sounded wonderful to be with Ivan for longer than just a weekend of uninhibited sex and sensual pleasure, my rational side told me I was a fool if I thought I could pull this off with him. There was no way I'd make it out unscathed. He would twist me up into all sorts of knots. Add in the fact I didn't deserve any kind of relationship with him... or with anyone really. My sins still hung heavy on my heart, and the self-flagellation was something I couldn't let go of just yet. Someday, maybe, I might be able to forgive myself for what I'd done four years ago.

I want so badly to have that... with you, Gabrielle.

When he'd said that second part to me, there was a definite yearning in his voice. I'd heard it clearly. I'd also sensed a loneliness in him. I think I picked up on it because feeling lonely was my favorite flavor these days. Could Ivan and I fill those lonesome feelings for each other? Was it right for me to give in to the desire I felt with him? Or was I fooling myself?

I'd guessed right about Ivan. He was a dominant even though I was certain he had mostly suppressed his natural inclinations whenever we'd been together thus far. I'd caught glimpses of the Dom behavior, of course, but then, coming from him, it turned me on wildly because Ivan Everley pushed every one of my sexual buttons.

I liked how Dom Ivan operated far too much.

Dominants can spot a submissive when they find one, so he'd guessed right about me, too. I couldn't hide my submissive nature from him any more than I could keep the urges buried any longer when I was with him like this—i.e., naked in his bed, weak from hours of attention from his cock and his hands and his mouth. I could barely hold on to a coherent thought, let alone keep my true desires under wraps.

He just knew.

"What are you asking me to—to do with you?" I still had to know. I needed to hear him lay it all out on the line before us. For me. I needed to hear it in order to go forward. I could literally feel my heart pounding in my chest as I waited for his response.

"I think you know, Gabrielle." He traced

down the side of my face with his finger, and then down my jawbone, further still to my chin before slipping onto the side of my neck to rest it over my pulse point. He pressed in, his finger sinking into the flesh of my neck. "I can feel the blood pumping under my finger. Your pulse is racing. Your perfectly flawless skin is flushed. The idea of my suggestion turns you on." He pressed his finger just a little harder. "Doesn't it, Gabrielle?"

Yes. I was in such deep trouble with this man.

His green eyes bored into mine as the pressure of his finger held me frozen, totally under his spell, powerless to turn away from his embrace any more than I could deny the truth in his words. That's all it took. Just one finger infused with the command of presence that Ivan Everley owned as certainly as he owned the handsome looks and the talented moves in the bedroom. Or art gallery storeroom. Or wedding reception dance floor. Or the interior of a sea plane.

As an involuntary shudder overtook me, the awareness of the strength of my attraction to him, to his wildly unexpected proposal, was very unnerving.

It was also so very tempting.

His response was to bring his lips closer and say, "Don't overthink. I know that's what you're doing." The press of his lips was as gentle as his kiss, firm but settling. With his tongue licking into me, he breathed, "Trust me, Gabrielle. Just trust me and say yes."

Damn, he was good.

How in the hell could I resist when we were naked in his bed with his lips on my skin, promising more pleasure than I'd ever known? An impossible feat for a woman much stronger than me, I am sure. I knew I wasn't ready to give an all-encompassing yes to his proposal, but I could give him an honest answer to his question.

"Yes, it turns me on, but how did you know, Ivan?" I managed to ask. I needed to know if I had a sign and arrows painted on my forehead. Flashing neon? >>>SEXUAL SUBMISSIVE<<<

My question stopped the kisses as he stared down at me. The intense look I was beginning to recognize was back. The rest of his fingers moved forward to take my neck in a possessive hold. "I didn't for certain, but I dearly hoped it was true. The clues were there during our first encounter at The National Gallery. The way you were in my arms when I made you come in that storeroom... Christ, Gabrielle." He licked his lips and his eyes flared. "You were perfectly submissive with me and I couldn't get you out of my head ever since that night. I thought about you for days and days. I wanted to see you again, but you disappeared and all I had to go on was 'Maria' wearing the green dress." His fingers left my neck, sliding down my arm to take my hand. He clasped it firmly and drew my arm up over my head with a sharp tug. My other arm got the same treatment until he had both wrists in his grip and me pinned below him. "I want you in that green dress again, too, because I definitely need a do-over of that night with you, Gabrielle."

"All right, we can do another date," I agreed quickly. His masterful dominance had me panting now and remembering all too well how he'd made me feel when he looked me over admiringly the first time—just as he was doing right now. Ivan knew how to make it feel so, so good.

"The way you surrendered to me when I

touched you, the sounds coming out of your mouth when you came." He stared intently at my lips before dragging his tongue over them slowly. "How you gracefully dropped to your knees prepared to suck me off like you wanted to do it."

"I did want to," I whispered, feeling myself flush with heat as he retold our first encounter.

"I know. I knew it then." His eyes flickered down at me, so beautifully green and deep as he studied me. "God, you're so... fucking sexy."

"You are too," I said shyly, "and I still can't believe what I did with you—a total stranger." And even now when recalling what I'd done with Ivan at The National Gallery that night, I was filled with shame at my weakness. Why did he affect me so? One look, one touch, one command, and I turned to putty in his hands. It had to be uniquely him I was certain.

"You've said that before, Gabrielle, and I hear you. I do. But honestly, I don't want you having shameful feelings about what we did together that night. In fact, I don't accept the idea at all. You did nothing wrong, kitten. Everything you did that night was perfect... to me. That's why it happened the way it did with us. Don't you see?" He pressed yet another erection into the side of my hip, and I had to give him props for stamina. The man was the mortal embodiment of a Greek god—an Eros—with a really big cock, which just kept going and going—"You felt comfortable with me that night... and we clicked, Gabrielle."

I nodded at him and enjoyed my view. Admiring his handsomeness, loving the weight of his lower body pressing into mine, the firm dominance he used with such ease. We clicked all right. Major clicking happened, that's for sure. I basically fell into his arms and let him do whatever he wanted to me in the gallery storeroom. Something I'd never allowed any other stranger to do within moments of being introduced. Ha! We were never even introduced. He thought I was Maria-the-Escort, and I got a kinky alter ego name for him. Mr. Ivanhoe. Embarrassment filled me yet again as I remembered. I'd been living such a guarded existence regarding men and dating since I'd come to London, that I had truly forgotten what it felt like to be desired intimately.

Ivan brought those feelings back for me while making it all feel so damn good; his offer was nearly impossible to resist.

"Just like you feel comfortable right now being restrained by my hands, wondering what I'll do next. You want me to do more and you'll surrender to it, too." Ivan continued watching me, the penetrating gleam in his eyes which appeared during sex only made me hotter.

Ivan reached his free hand into my borrowed smoking jacket tumbled on the bed beside us and drew out the silk-fringed belt. He dragged the dangling edge over my nipples, making me arch into the tingling sensation. "I want to use this, Gabrielle. I'd like to have your gorgeous body tied to my bed while I fuck you this time. Knowing you're going nowhere until I release you. Until I am done taking pleasure from the sight of you spread out and shaking from all the orgasms I'm going to give you. Until you've had as much as you can take and my cock has worked itself out to the point of fucking exhaustion," he said, watching me carefully, his body tense and tight looming above me.

I shuddered hard, again a completely involuntary action on my part. His simple words rendered me helpless when he started in with the directing. And he knew it, too, because he smiled darkly at my shuddering.

"Do you consent?"

"Yes," I whimpered, falling under the spell he'd cast on me with complete ease, letting him take control in this. Instinctively, I knew he would be better than anything I'd ever experienced before.

Green eyes blazed down at me with lust at my answer, and he wasted no time putting me into position. "You'll tell me what you need, Gabrielle?" he asked firmly while working on binding my hands together with the silk belt, testing the tautness before securing the silk to the headboard of his bed. "Green, yellow, or red. I'll hear you, whatever that may be." He deliberately brought his hands down to find my nipples, rolling them between his fingers, applying pressure until I felt the burn of sweet pain shoot through me and straight down to in between my legs. "If it's to back off, or if it's to give you more—just tell me." Ivan studied me intently to judge my response, for this was indeed a test.

I shuddered out a moan and arched my back, letting the rush of pleasure roll through as he eased off from pinching the nipples and switched to caressing my cupped breasts in each of his hands. "Yes, I'll tell you," I managed to gasp.

The green of his eyes seemed to flare once more at my agreement, the unmistakable gleam of triumph easy to see. I had pleased him very much, and the knowledge that I had done so switched on something inside me from which there could be no going back. This was a precipice and I'd just committed to going over the edge.

"And you want this with me, Gabrielle? You understand what your agreement means?"

I nodded slowly but deliberately, my heart surely on its way to flying out of my chest at the question, forcing me to acknowledge this thing we were starting together. We weren't just hooking up for sex anymore. Things had morphed into something new. There was so much more to this than a few fabulous orgasms for the both of us.

"What's your color right now, kitten?"

"Green." I felt a ripple of longing set free

inside me as I answered him, remembering something he'd said to me earlier: *Don't shut your eyes. I need to see those green beauties on me when you say yes.*

So, I kept my eyes on him as I gave him my agreement.

My soul felt free for the first time in longer than I could recall.

Chapter 2

Oh yes, an exchange of power was a great deal more, and then some. Especially when it was Ivan demanding it from me, knowing I was powerless to resist. He'd caught me now. My secret was no longer a secret to him. Rather, it was a bargaining chip between us. A negotiation tool for what we could offer to each other.

The potential of what it might mean for me to head back into territory that had been influential in a disastrous relationship which had left me emotionally devastated and adrift in my life. The D/s hadn't been the reason for my messed up history with Kent, but it'd definitely been a contributing factor in the poor decisions I'd made with him... and sadly tragic for others, I thought shamefully.

I truly didn't know if I was capable of delving into another D/s relationship and survive. A mysterious question to which I couldn't know the answer... until I did.

The circumstances were totally different with Ivan though. He was single. Yeah, a single guy who orders up an escort when he wants a date. Ugh. I didn't like those thoughts swimming around in my head, but I couldn't judge Ivan any more harshly than what I'd been party to with Kent. My deeds had been far worse.

Could I do this with him?

You want to.

I knew now I was about to find out.

The idea scared me as much as it excited me. No, that probably wasn't true. It excited me more.

He leaned back on his knees after he finished binding me, a satisfied expression creeping over his face. I wondered what he was thinking, even though I had a fairly good idea. He finally had me where he'd wanted me since that first time we'd been together. Ivan had me tied to his bed and I'd be there until he was good and ready to let me go. That sexual desert I'd been in? Well, the drought was very much o-ver. As in: Girl, you'd better brace yourself for some rain, cuz some big black storm clouds are headin' your way.

"You look so fucking sexy-beautiful right now, here, like this." He stared; his expression hard but not unaffected. He was affected all right. His cock was erect and ready to go again. Thank God, because I might die if he didn't touch me soon. I could say the same about him. Ivan was sexy-beautiful. Especially like this—hard and pulsing and about to start in on me.

"Open your legs and show me your divine cunt. I miss looking."

I didn't hesitate as I bent my left leg at the knee and slid my foot over and then repeated the same with the right leg. A feeling of immense pleasure washed through my body at the filthy command he'd just given me, coupled with the equally intense desire to let myself be taken into his care.

To give myself up to someone.

To Ivan.

He focused on my body, his eyes darting over what I'd just put on display at his request. "You have such a pretty pussy, Gabrielle. Almost as beautiful as your tits." He grinned devilishly and licked his lips slowly. "I said 'almost' because I don't think anything can compare to these," he said as he took a hold of a breast in each hand and squeezed. Hard.

I arched and gasped at the sharp jolt that flew through me, coming undone by the combination of the praise that he thought me beautiful tempered with the rough treatment. He soothed my nipples with firm sucking pulls until I was a writhing mess and soaking wet for him.

One hand made its way to between my legs and teased my clit with little pinches while his mouth continued to ravage my nipples. I welcomed the pulses that started to bring me toward what was bound to be a spectacular orgasm.

He stilled his hand. "Not yet, kitten. I own when you can come, and I want you begging me for it this time. I'll tell you when." He slid two fingers inside and stroked in and out before curling them up into my sweet spot and tugging.

"Ahh," I moaned, struggling to follow his command, the pleasure building forward again.

"You're very wet for me, kitten. I love how you're all soaking wet." He increased the pace of his fingers and the pressure on my G-spot so that the climax would come on quickly.

Kitten? It was a crazy thought to pop in my head in the moment of exactly what we were doing, but I realized I loved the sound of it rolling off his talented tongue. Sexy, yet adoring. God! It had to be straight-up Playboy-Bunny-era-sexism for Ivan to be using a name like "kitten" on me, but it was official, just about everything this man did turned me on and triggered my sexual buttons. Every last one of them.

There was no doubt he knew what he was doing.

Ivan's knowledge of a woman's body was something I didn't want to dwell upon, but in this moment made me supremely grateful he possessed. I floated along and let him take me to the mountain peak, mindful that he had yet to give me permission to come.

Oh God, I'm going to die.

And it would be a lovely fucking death. Quite literally.

I was already addicted to his touch on my skin, his natural scent, the weight of him when he was on top of me. I'd been wary of Ivan before for this very reason. I'd known I'd want him too much. Craving something too much had been my problem before, and even I could recognize how I was slipping back into the temptations of allowing my physical desires to rule me. It was me being reckless, taking risks.

But hell, it felt so damn good with him I couldn't deny what I wanted so desperately.

I nearly screamed when he took his fingers away. My eyes flared open in protest. But Ivan was right there, looking determined and watching me. "I know you want to come, but when you do, it will be at the end of my cock. I'll be in you."

Oh my God, yes, please. He was already sheathing himself while he said the words to me; the anticipation causing me to shudder at how he would feel again. I'd had the experience of him inside me now, of course, but not nearly enough. I needed another reminder. Or ten.

He mounted up, gripping my shins and bending me at the knees to make his way. He had me spread so open and exposed I felt the flush of embarrassment when I saw him looking me over. But the expression in his beautiful eyes quickly snubbed out any embarrassment on my part and replaced it with white hot desire. Ivan liked what he saw and made it clear. I could also tell this was an enactment of his kink. He wanted me restrained and spread out for him. It was how he liked to fuck.

But the thing was, I liked it too.

When he sank his cock into me, I let out a low keening moan of abandon, totally unable to keep quiet. He filled me up roughly, but it was exactly what I needed from him. Rough, hard, drilling penetrations that heated me from the inside out. I wanted to feel, and somehow Ivan made it all work so that was possible. He knew what to do, how to touch me, what to say to me in order to make it happen—to make me feel again. The painful grip on the back of my thighs, holding me open. The deep, hard strokes pounding as far into me as he could go. The harsh look on his face as he took what he wanted. *I own this body of yours when I have my cock in you.* Oh yes, I remembered what he'd said earlier. Remembered and noted.

Ravishment all the way.

"That's it, kitten, take it—take my big fucking cock inside your tight little cunt." He grunted on deep slides as he fucked me closer to the orgasm I so desperately wanted. With each heavy stroke of his cock into me, positioned just perfectly to drag against my clit, Ivan knew how to fuck properly.

I pleaded with him using my eyes, struggling to hold back the rush of the climax before it passed me onto the place where I wouldn't be able to suppress it no matter his command to wait for his permission.

He drilled me with his eyes burning green fire as his long hard cock did the same to my body, pushing into me so deeply I began to shake uncontrollably from the building pleasure.

"You ready to come?" he asked roughly, his voice thick with lust as he continued to fuck me relentlessly.

"Yeeeees, s-sir," I moaned desperately, barely able to answer as I clenched around him.

He frowned in displeasure and shook his head down at me. "Not sir, Gabrielle. Never sir with you and me. I want to hear 'my lord' shouted from your pretty mouth when you get there."

"I am there," I whimpered.

"Then you know what you need to do—"

His eyes flared wide, and he lost his words as I convulsed into the most spectacular orgasm of my life. I choked out, "My l-l-lord... my loorrrd," doing everything in my power to follow his command properly but couldn't be sure I'd performed to his precise specifications or not. He would let me know. That was part of what needed to be worked out between two consenting parties. I was just going on instinct with him so far and allowing him to dominate and control me during sex. I succumbed to the intensity of the pleasure he gave me and struggled to hold on to reality. I wasn't super successful because I was long out of practice. I got blissfully lost in the moment. It was so good.

I realized that Ivan came with me when I felt the sting of his bite at the base of my neck, his teeth surely marking me as he thrust hard and deep into me for the final few times to finish. I could feel the aftershocks of his cock jerking inside me, my inner muscles clutching and gripping him as my own rush flowed along. I didn't want it to be over, and yet it was.

We both breathed deeply and said nothing. He replaced his teeth with his warm tongue and soothed over the place where he'd bitten. He thrust lazily, still inside me and found my mouth, invading with his tongue there as he kissed me long and slow. In no hurry to stop, he just kissed me thoroughly, his cock still buried, filling me up with as much of him as I could be.

I knew one thing.

Ivan had made me forget for the first time. And for that reason alone, he was unique among all the men I'd known since falling from grace.

I want to hear 'my lord' shouted from your pretty mouth when you get there.

An interesting request, yes, but fitting considering he was one in real life and living a sort of lordly life in a mansion filled with priceless art. The mixture of his allure was over-the-top intoxicating for me. As we both breathed and came down from the high of incredible pleasure, Ivan seemed almost pained if I had to put a name to it. Just before reaching up to untie my hands, he looked longingly at me as he pulled himself slowly out of my body. He stayed on top of me though, still holding power over me with that searching expression he had sometimes as he rubbed first one wrist and then the other. Very gentle and caring touches that comforted me and helped me to believe I could trust him. My mind was far from quiet, though. Racing thoughts of *What just happened here?* or even more critical, *What now?*

I sensed Ivan was as deep in thought as I was about what had "just happened." D/s sex is different than straight sex, and we'd now crossed over the vanilla line most definitely. We both knew it, and yet we only each knew what we each knew.

I also didn't like to reflect on all the other women who'd been underneath Ivan Everley and realized my predecessors had to number in the hundreds.

"What is that frown for?" he asked softly.

"Hmm?"

"You frowned and your pretty eyes grew dark." He traced a finger to the corner of my eye, the gentle touch feeling extremely intimate to me.

"How many times have you done this, Ivan? What's my number in the long line of conquests?"

"Here? At Donadea? I already told you I don't bring women here. Your number is one."

"Seriously? I'm to believe that you've never had sex here before. Oh-kay—you know how that sounds, right? Really, fucking, implausible."

"It probably does sound implausible, but I can assure you it's the truth. I don't have any motive to lie to you, Gabrielle. In the few years since I inherited the place, I've used it pretty infrequently, mostly as a retreat away from the city. I've never had guests here at all. Apart from the staff who live and work here, it's only me. You really are the first."

"Well, that is... really surprising to hear, Ivan."

"I know, but there hasn't been anyone I've wanted to invite here before I found you," he said clearly, his green eyes twinkling at me. "I'd love for you to feel at home here and to stay for as long as you wish."

"You realize this is a lot more than just a weekend to get a leg over, as was suggested when you kidnapped me from the wedding."

"I know. And I thank you for being such an accommodating captive. You get an A plus for attitude and pluck, Miss Hargreave. But I'd hoped you were feeling much the same as me—this *has* become a lot more than just a shag weekend." He kissed me again because it's just what Ivan did whenever we talked. He kissed his way through our conversations. "Certainly been a lot more than that for me. Although, I should probably tell you you've been the very best leg over I can ever recall, Miss Hargreave."

"Why thank you for the compliment, Mr.

Everley." I liked hearing those words from him, I must admit. It was always wonderful to hear you were needed by another person. With Ivan I'd already heard it from him many times. And didn't that just make him all the harder to resist?

"Would you like a tour?" he asked in that way of his making it extremely difficult for anyone to say no. Charm came easily to Ivan and I could see how he used it to his advantage. I had to watch and learn if I had any hope of coming out of this experience in one piece.

"Of your art collection? Yes, of course." I was assuming this was what he was referring to, considering we'd done nothing even remotely art related since he'd brought me here under the guise of evaluating his paintings. Hah! I'd done some evaluating all right, but it had nothing to do with art. The art of sex maybe. If his painting collection stacked up against his skills in the bedroom, then I was going to have a hard time resisting coming back to Donadea. Who was I kidding? I'd never be able to resist returning when I knew how badly he wanted me here, plus the promise of uncovering art treasures hidden away since God only knew, if the small sample of what I'd glimpsed from moving room to room around his house was anything to go on then I was in for the motherlode. I had a strong feeling his collection was going to be newsworthy for the art world.

"I thought I'd take you outside first if you don't mind." He smiled and gave me a peck on the lips before sitting up on the side of the bed. His body was a thing of male beauty to ponder as he sat looking down at me. His sculpted back curved in my direction while his hips faced away and out of sight. Now he's being modest? Ivan's physique was on the larger side, but his muscles were lean rather than bulky. Beautiful. I resisted the urge to reach out and touch him. Anywhere would do—arm, thigh, shoulder, ass—all were good places to start if you asked me.

"I'd like that actually, and Mr. Finnegan said he had my clothes from last time, so I don't have to wear my dress from the wedding," I told him while pulling the sheet in from the side to cover my nakedness. I suddenly felt extremely vulnerable lying exposed and bare in his bed.

He stilled my hand to prevent me. "No, lovely thing, don't ever hide yourself from me when we are behind the door." His hand moved to a breast and clutched it before finding the nipple and giving it a tight pinch. The sharp sting forced a soft pleasurable moan from between my lips. "And that is exactly the reason right there. The sexy sound you gave me just now? I want to enjoy you and hear more of those sounds coming out of your mouth when I touch you." He smiled down at me, just one side of his mouth curling up. "And look at your beautiful body with my eyes. And to have you give to me your complete trust. I won't ever do anything you don't want me to do." His eyes flicked up and down the length of my body with purpose and appreciation. "All I can see is an incredibly beautiful creature who, I think," he paused with emphasis, "understands what I'd like from her."

Wow. He had no trouble expressing his desires. In a way, his directness relieved me. It was honest. The only way I could operate anymore. He'd said he wanted me submissive when we fuck. The "when we fuck" was key to his request. It was also the only time I would consider such a thing. Yeah, I'd learned that lesson the hard way.

"I understand, Ivan," I said, realizing he

needed a gesture of consent from me. "I know what you're asking of me."

"And?" His expression didn't change beyond the raising of an eyebrow and a slight tilt of his head.

"I think I need a little time to consider it," I said softly, steadying myself to tell him the rest, "because it's been a long time for me to be in this kind of... *relationship* with someone. I... I don't know if I can—or if I want—to do it again."

My words just seemed to make him more determined to convince me. I could see the wheels turning inside his pretty head as he switched on the persuasive charm and blasted me with it. "I'm sensing a dominant partner hurt you in the past, and did terrible damage to your trust, confidence, and most of all your self-worth. It ended badly, and while it's not my place to ask you to share any part of that story with me, you can if you ever want to. I'd love to know the name of the fucking shit so I can make his life a sodding misery for daring to harm a hair on your lovely head," he told me while touching a finger to my hair and tracing it firmly, and I might even say, *possessively* around my ear.

A smile threatened to break through at the thought of *my lord* Ivan protecting my honor by challenging Kent to a duel or something. He was now rubbing circles below my ear right against my neck, distracting me further. A deliciously sensual spot he'd discovered on my body. Ivan already knew where he should be touching me. How was this possible?

I was beyond understanding how it all would work. I didn't even want to try to figure it out. Ivan didn't seem to be worried a bit. He had enough confidence for the both of us. So, I let him plead his case. I leaned into his caress and allowed him to continue with his closing arguments most convincingly.

"I do know it's not good for you to deny yourself something you need, though. It also doesn't work that way. You cannot deny physical needs. You need the submission as much as I need the domination. And you're going to seek it out with someone at some point, and I believe that someone should be me, of course." He pressed his lips to the spot he'd been caressing with his thumb. "I'll take care of you here. We have a pretty damn perfect sexual connection already even without the kink, you know?" He stroked a single finger down from my lips, over my chin, down my neck, and then kept going determinedly until he reached a breast, stopping at my nipple. He circled the tip of his finger over my sensitive flesh, teasing it to attention with the added pinch between his thumb and forefinger. I couldn't help the intense jolt of pure pleasure that grabbed me any more than I could prevent the little moan that escaped my mouth. I could only observe the response of my body to his touch as my nipple budded up hard and tight under his fingers. "Am I right?"

"Yes." At least I wasn't lying to him. I could wholeheartedly agree that the sex was addictive even without kink. It was so good. So good.

"And Donadea is private and safe and don't forget the bonus of the art gig. You're going to be paid very well for a large job which could take an awfully long time to complete. It's the perfect arrangement in so many ways."

"But the university will be credited with the evaluation, not me. I won't be paid personally. My salary is from—I work for U of L—"

"Yes, you will be fucking paid, Gabrielle. My contract will be with you alone. I no longer have a contract with the university as of the morning after you left here the last time. Paul Langley called me out, chastised my stupid arse for sexual harassment of his student, and then dropped me as a donor to the university."

Whoa. I had no idea about Paul dropping Ivan. He'd mentioned before that Ivan was a big donor, so it must have hurt the budget a lot to cut him loose. I felt a twinge of guilt for turning him in to Paul, but he did proposition me and accuse me of being a sex worker. I truly believed he was mentally unstable. God, that situation with us the first time I came to Donadea was a complete clusterfuck of misunderstanding from start to finish.

"So... the art evaluation is a private contract between you and me?"

"It will be. I'll have the original redrawn and you can look it over tonight before you sign."

"Don't forget, I'm still a student in a graduate program. Any new works I bring in will still have to be certified by an official body like the university to be taken seriously in the fine art world. Nobody will accept the observations of a mere grad student. If I'm all on my own here, it won't be a sanctioned evaluation until you bring in someone official. Don't you want this to be an official cataloguing of the Donadea collection, Ivan?"

"When you put it like that," he said thoughtfully, stroking his stubbled chin in a way that made me insanely jealous of his hand, "I'm only more determined that it just be you, Gabrielle." He gave me a devious little wink, making me note his successful fake-out. "The fact that you're so passionate about protecting the provenance of the Donadea collection before you've even had any kind of look at it, and willing to forgo payment even, just further convinces me that you're the only person I want for this job. Can I make myself any clearer on the matter?"

"Wow, that's a lot of confidence in someone you don't even know beyond a friendship with your cousin's new bride."

"Not really. Paul Langley sent you here in the

first place. He said you were uniquely suited for this job, in fact. He chose you. We may not be on the best of terms at the moment, but I trust department chair, Paul Langley, as the go-to-guy for knowing who to entrust with a valuable collection of bloody fucking art."

Stifling the urge to laugh was impossible. It slipped out of me. He made me smile and laugh with the stiff-upper-lipped, civilized British sarcasm he used so liberally in his speech. Even more when arguing a point—which, I might add, he did often. It seemed that Ivan had no problem at all offering up plenty of arguments for why his way was the right and correct decision. Must be the politician in him. *My lord* indeed. A lord in life and in personality really existed on the earth. Somehow, I'd found a unicorn. Or... the unicorn had somehow found me.

Just listening to Ivan talk was enjoyable to me for some reason. That voice of his... A mercurial beast in a *Brunello Cucinelli*. A sophisticated savage. A Greek god—my Eros asking for permission to worship at my temple. When he spoke, the words that came out of his mouth were something just so very beautiful—

Words saying, I was sexy and gorgeous. Words commanding me to take him inside me and submit to his desires. Words so very filthy, but also perfectly placed in divine moments of deliciously dirty fucking. Words kissed over my body and caressed into my skin reverently. Words laughed back at me for something witty I'd said. Words of compliment, but also of the most brutal honesty.

"The little laugh you just gave me tells me all I need to know, Miss Hargreave. Thank you for that. Because now I know you're going to sign that contract, and then we can negotiate the rest. I will require a non-disclosure for privacy reasons. Which will cover the collection's contents as well as your relationship with me, and also extend to any time you're here in residence at the estate. You can't discuss any of it with anybody. The non-disclosure takes precedence over the contract for the art evaluation, I'm afraid. I hope you won't have a problem with that." He stared down at me, probably trying to read my reaction to his requirement of a non-disclosure agreement for being here at Donadea, regardless of what I was doing. Evaluating his art collection or working off the sexual tension surrounding us like a brewing storm cloud which never quite blew clear through. I'd be doing both if I accepted and signed. Yes, maintaining his privacy here at this lovely aristocratic oasis perched among the wildness of the North Irish coast was indeed extremely important to Ivan Everley. Even I could deduce that significant fact at this juncture just from our limited encounters with each other up till now. God, the night I showed up here in the rain and surprised him... He was so enraged at his privacy being breached, mistaken identity or not. It was a trigger for him. One I'd have to remember.

But it was important for me to make one more thing clear to him before he started asking for signatures on contracts. He needed to know. "Ivan, as long as *you* understand that the submission happens behind the door for me. It won't ever cross over into the rest of my life, or my work. During sex is the only time I feel the desire—when I feel like giving up control to another person. The only time."

I watched Ivan's eyes flare before going dark and predatory. He leaned down farther and boxed me in, his hands planted firmly on the bed, even with my shoulders like a panther about to spring.

A gorgeous wild panther I wanted to pet and lick and have purring against my leg. I could feel the body heat radiating off him and smell the sex in the air from what we'd been doing for the last hour. And in spite of all the orgasms he'd already given to me in that time, I could still be aroused by him, as evidenced by the delicious shiver that rolled through me from him devouring me with his gorgeous green eyes. His effect upon me sexually was immense, and I was certain he knew it.

His harsh expression softened. "Perfect answer, kitten. Now I think I'll have a shower and dress myself before I consider what else I might like to do with you behind the door. I really would like you to see more of my home than just this bedroom." He gave me a final thorough kiss to my lips, and also a lick and a suck to each of my breasts, murmuring, "Such spectacular tits," before pulling away and boasting a pleased grin on his handsome face.

I suppose my admission of being submissive only "when we fuck" had made his day.

He was still grinning smugly when he

sauntered into the bathroom after that snazzy little speech, his tight bare ass looking mighty fine from my view as I tilted my head to admire. What a gorgeous man he was, and amazingly he didn't act like most guys who knew they were hot and tried to pull off being artificially humble. Ivan just behaved like a man who was completely comfortable in his own skin. A confident and easy man. Must be nice, I thought—with a bit of envy thrown in—to feel so confident.

As I got up from his bed and drew on the cerulean blue silk smoking jacket he'd gifted to me, I decided I wouldn't tell him his habit of calling me "kitten" had a very nice effect on me.

Mr. "my lord" Everley would just have to work for the right to that knowledge.

Chapter 3

Ivan left me in privacy to shower and dress, asking me to meet him in front of the pool house when I was ready. I thought it was considerate of him to give me some alone time, because I was feeling more than a little self-conscious after all the sex. Not shy, so much, but rather more of an awareness of what we'd been doing *a lot* of since last night. It had been a long time for me, and I had the delicious aches and soreness to prove it.

After a luxurious shower taken in the equally luxurious and recently remodeled marble bathroom, I remembered to give thanks about being so careless as to leave my muddy clothes behind when I was here before. That and Mr. Finnegan's laundering skills had me dressed in the same jeans and emerald green shirt I'd worn the night Ivan found me lost on the road, just sans the mud. Underwear and socks included. He'd even polished up my leather ankle boots and laid out a new toothbrush for me. I really needed to find out what Mr. Finnegan's guilty pleasures were so I could buy him a thank you gift. He was the kindest man.

I realized as I checked myself in the mirror that Ivan was going to get a dose of me au naturel today. No makeup, and damp hair that had been combed out and French braided into one braid on the side. I found a hair band in the pocket of my jeans, miraculously still in there after laundering. There wasn't a thing I could do about it, though, and I decided if he didn't like me this way, then it was going to be his problem. He'd seen me a mess already anyway after our swim and he didn't seem to mind. In fact, Ivan went out of his way to tell me I was beautiful. I switched off the light in the bathroom and set out to find him, thinking it was really nice to be told you were beautiful. I wanted to believe it. So badly, I wanted to believe it. My problem wasn't the beauty on the outside though. I could deal with that. It was the inside part of me I doubted. I'd been very selfish and sinful once, and for that I still must atone.

I retraced my way from what I remembered this morning when we went to the pool house for our swim. As I made my way down, I allowed myself to really take in the art displayed everywhere around me. The walls were covered and so was the grand staircase. In the daylight I could see the beauty in the paint, and it made me giddy. My throat got tight and I had to forcibly keep my excitement under control because there was so much. I knew I could get lost in these works, and it had nothing to do with the oh-so-charming and sexy owner. He helped of course, but Ivan's art collection could hold its own no problem whatsoever.

My eyes found a painting on the stairwell with a subject I recognized immediately. It was a slightly different version of my favorite Mallerton on display in The National Gallery. What we call a *simulacrum* in the art trade. The young bride on the white horse—Mrs. Gravelle. Same beautiful girl with long dark hair in her wedding finery riding a magnificent white stallion decked out for the occasion. Only in this version, the pose was altered somewhat for the horse and rider. I stared in awe. Holy shit, I was looking at another Mallerton which wasn't even in the archives. I found his signature and leaned closer to scrutinize the structure of the letters without the benefit of my glasses. It absolutely presented as authentic from first glance. The painting was in need of general cleaning, but otherwise perfectly gorgeous decorating the grand stairwell of Donadea. I wanted so badly to take it with me back to London for further examination. It would be a dream job to bring this version of Mrs. Gravelle back to her original glory. And this was just *one* single painting of many, many more just waiting for some attention. I was still reeling from the discovery of the Mallerton at Hallborough this weekend at the wedding. The family portrait of Sir Jeremy and Lady Georgina Greymont with their children.

That made two uncatalogued works of Mallerton's discovered in as many days. Crazy. I might need to bring in someone to help me, or at least ask Ben to come and take initial inventory photos—

"There you are," Ivan called up from the bottom of the stairs. "I wondered if you got lost, and now I can see you've found something to distract you." He looked gorgeous smirking up at me in worn jeans and a cream linen shirt, and I couldn't help imagining him as he'd been with me just an hour ago—without the expensive clothes that he wore so well. That was the thing about Ivan. He wore everything, or nothing, so very well.

"Mrs. Gravelle is here on your wall. This is a Mallerton in your house, Ivan, and nobody knows it exists except for me," I told him as I continued to study the painting in awe.

"Ahh, you like that one, do you? Good, right?"

"I wouldn't use 'good' to describe this discovery," I answered sarcastically without looking at him. The horse was depicted mid-step with his front leg held high, while Mrs. Gravelle sat serenely in her ivory wedding dress looking beautiful and happy. I wanted so badly to know more about her. "Please tell me you know something about the woman in this painting," I said pleadingly. "There's a different version of this portrait in The National Gallery and it's my favorite Mallerton out of all of them. The bride, the white horse, the romance of it all—everything about it..."

My words were utterly lost as I tried to explain. It was impossible to make anyone understand the significance of what I'd just discovered in his house if they didn't already know fine art. Mallerton wasn't even constrained in part to the realm of fine art. He surpassed it. His works were straight-up national treasures.

"A painting like this one is a conservator's dream," I finished lamely, still unable to drag my eyes away from the canvas. I knew I sounded like a lovesick fool just from hearing myself babbling on, but I couldn't help it.

I could tell I amused him, and he liked having me interested in his paintings, though. I couldn't blame him really. He'd gotten his way—and me—over to Donadea again to take a look at his artwork.

And hoped to have me in his bed doing... him.

I wasn't completely sure if that was right, but it seemed pretty accurate from my perspective. I knew I liked being with him, and I did trust he was being honest when he shared with me what he wanted. I found his directness pleasing. We were both attracted to each other. I had to agree the sex was off the charts, and the arrangement would be private. He'd said nobody would have to know, to my great relief. And legally, I couldn't talk about anything, which made it even easier. Explaining to Brynne and Ethan, not to mention my father, I was being kinked by Ivan Everley was not on my list of things to do. Ever.

"The bride was a relation of my great-great-grandmother. They were very close, almost like sisters I've been told. She's in another painting hanging in the main gallery—of ladies playing cards." He had come up the stairs and was now behind me, his hands finding their way easily onto my hips. I had to admit, his touch was nice—comfortable—not demanding at all. It made me feel as if he was genuinely glad to have me with him. Not the typical morning after "I'll call you" right before heading out the door. I was coming to find out Ivan was nothing like what he appeared on the surface, and it only helped my trust to grow even further.

"Sounds amazing. I can't wait to see it." A painting of Mrs. Gravelle and other ladies playing cards? Did Mallerton paint it as well? I sighed impatiently, eager to start my evaluation, and knowing I was on the threshold of significant discovery. Ivan had a remarkable collection of art and I'd only seen mere bits and pieces of it so far.

"The one to ask would be my gran, but she lives in Paris nearly all the year now and her traveling days are behind her. She is the only person who I know of to take even a passing interest in the family artworks in decades. My grandfather, who died before I was born, certainly didn't according to her," he said dryly.

"Your grandmother lives in Paris?"

"She does indeed."

"She is French?"

"Well, yes, in the sense she's a French citizen having been born and raised there. But she is

Russian by blood. Both her parents fled Russia as children with their families during the revolution. In fact, she's a Romanov descendant on her mother's side."

I froze against him. "A Romanov descendant, as in the Russian royal family Romanov?" No wonder he needed a professional to delve into his painting collection and advise him. There was no telling what sorts of treasures were buried here if Ivan had Russian czars in his family tree. "Is that why you have a Russian name of Ivan?"

"Minor royalty descended from a royal house with no country and no status for more than a century, and yes, my name came from my gran. It was her father's name as well. Her surname was Ivanova before she married my grandfather and became an Everley." He nuzzled my neck with his lips from behind, the rough stubble of his unshaven beard making me shiver deliciously. "I should take you to Paris to meet my gran. I'd wager you and her would get on famously with your love of art and paintings. In fact, she's been scolding me for ages to get someone in here to organize the collection. I should ring her up and tell her I've finally managed it."

Paris with Ivan. That would be hard to turn down if he ever really wanted to do it. "Well, I agree with your gran. You *should* have asked for a conservationist to come here ages ago as she suggested. From the tiny bit I've seen since I came downstairs, I am salivating to see what else you've got stashed away in this house." I shook my head and wiggled around to face him.

"Ahh, I like the sound of that. You salivating for *more*," he said suggestively. "I don't think you'll be disappointed if just this little painting here can wind you up." He gently took hold of my chin and tilted my face up to his. "There are plenty of other paintings for you to see, but I very much want to show you something outside first. May I, Gabrielle?"

His request was so sincere it would have been impossible to tell him no, plus I'd enjoyed everything he'd done with me since he'd brought me here. Ivan had taken care of me in more ways than one, and I was sure whatever he had awaiting us outside would be well worth it. The paintings I was dying to look over had already been here at

Donadea for decades, and another day wouldn't change them. I could tell whatever he wanted to show me was important to him.

And then it happened.

Suddenly I wanted nothing more than to please him. It was as startling as it was powerful. A driving force within me. I was falling into my role just as easily as if it had always been like this between us.

"Yes," I said. "Please show me."

The expression on his handsome face along with the kiss he gave me let me know that I'd made him happy, too.

"FIRST YOU TIE ME to your bed, and then you blindfold me. You *are* quite kinky, Lord Everinghamwich." I couldn't resist the tease as I let him lead me along a path somewhere on his vast property. He'd taken us in his Willys Jeep for part of the way, pointing out various landmarks to mark the edges of the estate. I knew I wouldn't remember the finer details. Donadea was big, I deduced that much. The countryside of Northern Ireland was some of the most scenic I'd ever experienced in the UK, so I could understand Ivan's attachment to this place. If I owned a gem like Donadea, I'd want to sneak away from London every chance I got.

"You have no idea, Miss Hargreave, of the depths to which my kink abounds, but I have hope of enlightening you on the matter," he said silkily, delivering the perfect comeback capable of shutting me up.

Now why was that statement giving me tummy flutters when less than twenty-four hours ago I wanted to brain him with a bat? He had the charm factor down for sure. I felt excited as he worked on untying the blindfold, which was really just a linen table napkin he'd tied around my head, wondering what he wanted to show me so badly.

I gasped when I discovered exactly what it was.

A garden folly with a round stone gazebo-like building set amongst the prettiest natural landscape set alongside a small pond, complete with a table and chairs and what appeared to be a picnic lunch. "This is just—"

Words were impossible as I walked toward the pond's edge and saw fat Japanese koi in flashes of orange, white, and yellow swimming lazily toward me, probably in hopes of food. The scene was so quintessentially romantic it literally screamed "Jane Austen novel." And I had my own version of Mr. Darcy charming the pants off me. For reals. "You arranged this picnic for us?"

"Do you like it?" he asked from behind me.

I spun around and faced him, unable to do more than just shake my head at him.

"No?" His expression gave nothing away, and I knew it was time to tease him some more.

"Yeah, I'm sorry, but I don't like it." I turned away and walked back toward the fish and waited, wondering how long it would take him to react.

He came up behind me again but didn't put his hands on me this time. "Not a fan of picnics?" he asked quietly.

"I said I didn't *like* it, but only because I really

LOVE it." He grabbed me and tickled my ribs, his big body pressing into mine with familiarity. "Like and love—not the same!" I screeched, trying to get away from his tickling fingers. I got in a few good digs of my own before he hauled me over his shoulder, trapping me and laughing in that deep sexy way of his. I dug my fingers into his own ribs as he manhandled me, hoping I was getting to him. I think so because he started to move faster toward our picnic, probably to get me off him sooner. I was laughing too when he dropped me down into my chair, happy to see I'd affected him, even if only a little. It was all so fun with him. Being here with Ivan was fun, and I knew I couldn't say no to having more time like this with him. He wanted more? Hell, I needed more.

Chapter 4

Like and love—not the same.

Her words struck me hard. What was I even doing with this woman? I don't think I had a goddamn clue. Operating on pure instinct, I just knew I wanted her. I knew being with Gabrielle like this, with her happy and playful, made me feel really fucking good. I didn't want to overanalyze, but it had been so long since I'd felt this good with someone, it wasn't easy recognizing the sensation. For now, I'd just have to hold on to the good feelings and hope I wasn't being a bloody fool over a woman—for what would not be the first time in my life.

Once I was finally seated across from her, and could think for more than five seconds without the distracting desire to fold her over our lunch table and fuck her into next week, I managed to serve the food and pour the drinks without incident.

"You do feed your dates well, Lord Everley, I'll give you that," she said over a bite of roast beef sandwich, "this is delicious." It was very charming to me she didn't understand how names and titles worked. Being American, she had no reason to know, so I couldn't fault her reasonable mistake.

"I wouldn't call you a date." She was so much more. The two of us were miles beyond dates, even if she didn't know it yet.

"Well, what would you call me then?" she asked saucily.

"A challenge." And she was that. I'd barely accepted the fact she was the same woman Ethan wanted to introduce me to months ago. Fate at work. "You are the loveliest challenge to ever put me through my paces, Miss Hargreave." She looked down shyly and my cock stirred in appreciation. Just one small submissive gesture from her and my inner Dom was running rampant with what I wanted to do with her. I already knew she was a person who dealt in truths, but I wondered if she too believed in fate. Did she have any idea how attracted I was? I doubted it, and I wasn't planning on sharing that bit of information with her just yet either, because I had her now. Gabrielle Hargreave was all mine whether she knew it or not.

"Touché, Lord Everley, good answer. I like being a challenge." She smiled beautifully before licking her lips in a way that should be illegal.

I groaned and remembered how good her lips felt on my skin earlier—wrapped around me, kissing up the length of my—

"Did I distract you just now, Lord Everley?" she asked coyly, knowing full well what she was doing to me. Such a tarty tease. Later on, I'd show her just how *distracted* I was. Turnabout was fair play after all.

"I should let you know that Everley is my

surname, not my title. No Lord Everley in Parliament."

Her face lit up in surprise. "Is that what you do, Ivan? For a job? You're a member of Parliament. In the House of Lords?"

She really had no idea was clearly apparent. "Why yes, I do sit in the House of Lords. I try my best to serve the nation in those areas I can be of some small help."

"Jesus..." She looked shocked. "And you're descended from the last czar of Russia, too."

I suppose my creds did sound hideously pompous to someone like her, but nobody could change the circumstances of their birth. I'd lived with it for thirty-four years and it wasn't going away until I was dead. "What did you think I did for work?"

"Oh, I don't know, maybe ruling over the villagers in between all those state dinners that barons and dukes must have to attend. And maybe there should be some time in there for counting your piles of money, giving speeches to the historical society, and passing out the trophies at the local dog show?" She tilted her head at me and bit one side of her luscious bottom lip. I resisted the urge to stroke my finger across it and imagined replacing my finger with the tip of my cock instead. An even nicer image...

"Quite the job description you've given me. Sorry to disappoint, but I've never ruled over any villages, nor am I a member of any historical societies I know of. I do give the occasional speech but it's always work related. I only attend a state dinner when I can find no excuse to get out of it, and I have to invest my money wisely so I can continue to live here instead of some dreadful hovel beneath my station," I said absurdly. "Oh, and banks are the best place for the piles of money needing counting." I grinned at her. "As a bonus, the bank will count it for you too."

She laughed at my sarcasm. "This is unreal. You're a politician."

"It wasn't a thing I aspired to, but rather an obligation of sorts handed down to me. But ironically, serving as a member of Parliament suited me far better than I ever thought it would," I told her honestly.

"Oh, how so?" she asked with genuine

interest. It was refreshing to be with a person who didn't know anything about me, and who didn't judge me based on my status or my past achievements. Another point in her favor from where I sat. I wasn't going to let her out of my sight until I was certain she was hooked.

"Archery."

"As in bow and arrow?"

"The very same, Miss Hargreave."

"Ahh, I remember now." She nodded enthusiastically. "Brynne mentioned you were involved with the Olympics in London and that you did a sport. So, archery, that's cool. I've always admired the skill it takes to shoot so accurately, but I know next to nothing about it beyond Katniss in Hunger Games."

"I'd be happy to give you some lessons if you want to give it a go to see if you do like it. I can't promise you'll be as good as Katniss, but you *will* know proper stance and set-up when I'm done with you." *Which might be never.* The idea of teaching her thrilled me.

"I would love a lesson, but how does your

archery help you be suited to work in parliamentary politics?"

"Astute question." I gave her another wink. "When I was younger, I competed nationally for Britain. The Olympics are something I am passionate about. Sport and fitness are big business in the UK, and there are legal standards to be adhered to, school athletics guidelines, professional sports teams' regulatory standards, health and fitness schemes for educational advancement, and a great deal more. Most of my work in Parliament is devoted to legislation in those areas as Minister of Culture, Digital, Media, and Sport. It's where I can contribute my expertise, so it makes the most sense. You wouldn't want to put me in charge of European Union policy, or stem cell research, I'd be useless."

"Jesus. So, on top of being a cabinet minister in Parliament, a blood descendant of the Romanovs, you're also an Olympian?"

"I participated in three different Olympic games before retiring from competition. My recent involvement with the London games was as commentator and ambassador for the sport only."

"Impressive. Did you take home any medals at your three Olympics?"

"A few." I saw no reason not to be evasive with her, so I did my best to answer truthfully without offering extra information. She didn't seem to be intimidated when it came to questions, I'd noticed.

"How many Olympic medals do you have?"

"Eight. And before you ask the next question, it's four bronze, two silver, and two gold." I didn't mention the World Archery Championships I'd earned.

"Of course, you have eight Olympic medals on top of everything else, Ivan." She just shook her head in disbelief and smirked at me from behind her wineglass.

In a way, I was reluctant to tell her about my past. The information age we lived in made certain no stone was left unturned for a celebrity, be it their professional or private life. The tabloids also shared their erroneous findings with anyone who might buy a newspaper or two. Sex scandals were the most sought after by the paparazzi and sold massive amounts of papers. I was no saint to be fair, but the vile lies printed about me were nothing short of pure calculated revenge. I knew who instigated it, and I knew why. The thing was, the cat was out of the bag now and there was no turning back. Gabrielle could do an internet search and find out a lot more about me. And right next to my archery stats would be some sordid shit I hated for her to know. I went the denial route instead. "Enough about me and my circumstances of birth, I want to hear about you, Gabrielle. How did you find your way here all the way from Santa Barbara?"

I KNEW IT WAS COMING. I'd been asking Ivan a lot of personal questions, so it was only fair for him to be curious about me. I decided to go with the easy stuff first.

"Well, I grew up in Santa Barbara with my mom, who was American, but I was born in London and have a UK passport. My dad is a British citizen. He's the Chief Superintendent for the Southwark Division at New Scotland Yard. My younger sister, Danielle, and I visited him in London during our school holidays and summers over the years. He met my mother when she was like nineteen years old. My grandparents were diplomats who moved the family to London when my mom was a teenager. My mom and dad fell in love, or more accurately, she fell pregnant with me. My grandparents were not happy about their marriage and they interfered... more than they should have. My mother left England after two years, returning to California pregnant with my sister. My grandparents were killed in a car accident a few years later. Mom married my stepfather and had my brother Blake. My sister recently graduated from university and now studies fine art and design in Los Angeles. My brother goes to UC Santa Barbara, the same school where I did my undergrad, and lives at home with his dad, my stepfather. I came to London to study art and learn conservation. My mom died suddenly three years ago, and I'll never live in the US again."

I took a deep breath as I finished my oration and kept up my game face. It was better this way. Profoundly ashamed of the real reason I'd left home, wasn't something I was willing to share, especially when I could barely deal with my guilt now, years later. I was, for lack of a better term, deeply fucked up over what I'd done.

He nodded slowly after listening to my rambling speech, giving me his full attention. I was certain he'd absorbed every detail. I'd already experienced Ivan as a thoughtful listener, much to my surprise. Again, he went against the norm—at least for me he did.

"I'm very sorry about your mum. I lost mine suddenly, too." He paused before delivering the worst part of the news. "When I was six." He shrugged helplessly. "Pissing drunk driver took to the road and hit them head-on. They never stood a chance."

"They? Your father too?" I asked, thinking six

was a horrifying age to be orphaned. No wonder he was a little rough around the edges. Any guy would be affected without a mother's love and gentling influence from such a young age. I thought of Ethan and saw some of the same hardness he had also in Ivan. Brynne had told me that Ethan lost his mom when he was like four years old in a car accident. Ethan and Ivan were cousins... While my heart was hurting for the little six-year-old Ivan, imagining how hard it must have been for him growing up with no mother, it dawned on me to wonder if he and Ethan had shared the same tragedy.

He shook his head. "No, my father wasn't with her. She was with her sister and they were coming home from their grandfather's funeral..."

"Ethan and Hannah's mother was your mum's sister?" What a sad, sad connection for Ivan and his cousins to share. It was understandable though. Their relationship, the closeness, the family loyalty—they were all deeply bonded over the same tragic loss.

He nodded in the affirmative, the expression on his face showing me it was still a painful memory for him. I wanted to comfort him but had no idea what I could possibly say that wouldn't sound dismissive.

"That's incredibly tragic, Ivan. I'm so sorry about your mum, but I am glad you still had your dad," I offered lamely, before instantly regretting it. Ivan's whole body stiffened, and his jaw hardened in what could only be interpreted as anger. I'd said the wrong thing apparently, and I felt badly for bringing up sad memories for him. "I'm sorry," I whispered, wishing for an *un-ring* button on that bell, and maybe an accompanying mute button for my big mouth. Ivan's father was definitely off the list of acceptable conversation topics.

"Let's change subjects, shall we? There has to be something more pleasant for us to talk about." He smoothly shifted focus to the landscape beyond us and took a sip of his wine. When he moved his eyes back to me, the sexy, sophisticated, confident Ivan had returned. Just that fast. He had learned how to turn it on and off at will. I was struck with the urge to hug him, but I just sat in my chair sipping my wine and looked out at the beautiful green landscape of his beloved Donadea instead. I could feel his eyes on me. Staring. What did he see in me?

"So, you were born in London but raised in California?"

I nodded and turned my eyes back to him, glad that our awkward moment had passed.

"Well, that certainly explains the accent. I remember being surprised you weren't a native that night I picked you up on the road. Turns out, you really are a native. Just another perfect example of how things are not always as they appear on the surface." He picked up my hand from the table and stroked over my knuckles with his thumb. "I want you to remember that as you learn more about me." That last bit from him sounded sincere and struck me as a significant point for him. Was Ivan scarred from a painful past like me? Something to do with his father perhaps? He appeared so confident, but I would never forget how paranoid he'd behaved when I surprised him here that horrible night in the rain. He was a man who guarded his privacy fiercely, so I imagined he probably had his reasons, and I respected him for it because I was basically the same way. I totally got it.

"You already are so very different from what I thought at first anyway," I told him. "And in a good way, Ivan."

He flashed a gorgeous smile at hearing my words and it made my belly take a little dive. "So nice to hear, because I very much want your good opinion, Gabrielle, after the disastrous start we had. I hope you really believe that about me."

"I do. Other than kidnapping me from Ethan and Brynne's wedding, you've been an excellent host this time around, and you do feed me so very well." Sarcasm was easy with him, and he seemed to like it from me.

"I am giving it my best, but should I be worried about the fact your dad is a MetPol chief?"

I couldn't resist nodding. "I would be if I were you. I mean... kidnapping the chief superintendent's daughter can't be twisted into a good story no matter how you try."

"Are you going to tell him?" he asked cautiously. It dawned on me he might actually be worried about my dad. I could have kept on goading and made him really squirm, but I didn't want to. It was because Ivan "kidnapping" me to bring me back to Donadea had been the absolute right thing to do.

"Probably not," I said coyly, "if you continue to be *nice* to your incarcerated guest, that is."

He laughed and stared at my mouth, the desire between us sparking to life all in an instant. I wanted him again. "Where have you been hiding, Miss Hargreave? I so needed to find you a long time ago," he said wistfully, "and I promise to be very *nice* to you for as long as you stay."

I gulped. *London. I've been hiding in London.* "I've been right out in the open actually, just working and going to school," I said with a smile.

To give him the truthful answer to his question was too painful. There was no way I could share with him yet. Maybe in time I'd be brave enough and find my courage.

That is if this weekend evolved into anything further between Ivan and me after it was over.

Chapter 5

"So, are you finished eating and ready for the next stop on this tour?" I indicated to her luncheon plate.

"I am finished, but I bet my *tour* the night we met at the Mallerton Gala was better than whatever you have for me," she teased with a tempting little grin, managing to find a joke in my words and make me hard at the same time. She was so quick with her mouth.

Which just led to thoughts of some really filthy

things we could do with her pretty mouth. And she would—later. "Without a doubt, your tour wins, but I really do want to introduce you to my friends, and I think you'll like each other a great deal."

She made a shocked face. "You have friends?"

Very, very few that I can trust. "That's it. On your feet, Miss Hargreave, or I'll be throwing you over my shoulder again."

She got up from the table and came over, snaking her arms around to my back and hugged me. It was a surprise, and yet it wasn't. Gabrielle was so unpredictable, but it was one of the most refreshing things about her.

I glanced down at her and asked, "What did I do to deserve a hug from you just now?"

She spoke against my chest, her soft cheek warming my skin right through my shirt. "It was rude of me, and I'm sorry. Of course, you have friends, Ivan."

What I wouldn't give for a room with a door right now so I could show her how much I really appreciated her gesture. The great outdoors would have to do, and if people saw and thought I'd lost my mind, then so be it. I almost didn't know what to say to her. Nobody had ever apologized to me so sweetly before. At least not anytime in recent memory, and I wanted her to understand how much it meant to me.

"You're so bloody sweet." I took her face in my hands and kissed her slowly, loving the taste of the wine on her tongue as it tangled with mine. I wanted to crawl up inside her again, she felt so good against me.

Like fucking perfection fitting against my body as if we were interlocking parts of a puzzle.

The sound of a throat clearing behind us killed the interlude, much to my frustration.

Gabrielle jerked back as I turned to face the offender. Marjorie. One of the few people who didn't annoy me, so I couldn't be an arse to her for interrupting. It wasn't her fault I was outside with my tongue down Gabrielle's throat. A few moments later and she might have caught me being downright indecent, so there was that.

"Sorry for the intrusion, Ivan, but I saw the Willys and thought to come ask if you needed something." Marjorie's eyes moved quickly over Gabrielle, who had two fingers up to her lips and a clearly embarrassed blush on her face. So damn beautiful with her hair moving in the breeze, I could hardly take my eyes off her to address Marjorie's question.

"No, I don't need anything, but I should introduce you to Miss Hargreave from the University of London who'll be working here with us to get the art catalogued." I moved in close and put my arm around Gabrielle, I suppose making a show that she was someone important to me. Marjorie caught on quickly, which was no surprise. There was good reason we got on so well. "Gabrielle Hargreave, Marjorie Palmer, my estate manager and probably the sanest person I know."

"Miss Hargreave, welcome to Donadea. It's a good thing for you to get all those paintings sorted for Ivan, indeed." She offered her hand.

Gabrielle seemed to snap out of her embarrassment and shook hands politely. "Thank you, Marjorie. Donadea is breathtaking, and please, call me Gaby."

Marjorie grinned knowingly as she turned to

go, probably on her way to search out some gossip from Finnegan on catching me snogging a woman at Donadea. "I'll leave you in peace then, and nice to have met you, Gaby. Please, carry on."

A huge sigh from Gabrielle broke the silence. "Well, that was fun. Second time today we've been busted by your staff. Who else is left here to meet? And do I have to meet them topless in the pool or caught in a compromising position with you because it just really sucks!" She stomped her foot for emphasis.

"Marjorie likes you, and we've already established that Finnegan adores you," I said calmly. That she was adorably annoyed was sexy as hell to me. Being worried about her reputation amongst my staff showed she had some integrity. Gabrielle was nothing like the women I'd been with in the past, and the more time we spent together, the more this fact was finally sinking through my thick skull. It was probably the reason I'd been so desperate to bring her back here. Alone. I wanted her dependent upon me with no other options than to give in to what I believed would be good between us. My subconscious knew it the night we met. Too bad my inner Mr. Hyde appeared when she showed up on my doorstep. I fucked up that night... about as badly as one can, but here was a second chance to make it up to her.

I grinned at her fuming expression, loving the feistiness and the flash of defiance. It only made me crave the pleasure to be had in taming her. The sex was so fucking outstanding with her, but it wasn't just the sex that I needed. With Gabrielle I needed more than what she could do for me sexually. And that was the difference. More. I just wanted *more* from her without even knowing exactly what *more* exactly meant yet.

I couldn't remember ever wanting more... from anyone.

"I don't even want to imagine what Mr. Finnegan and Marjorie are thinking about me. How am I going to work here at Donadea and be taken with any level of credibility after what they've both witnessed us doing knowing we're having sex all the—"

I slammed my lips down on hers to stop the tirade. It worked, and in a few seconds, I had my submissive sexy kitten moaning softly against my tongue. Kitten was the perfect descriptor for her, too. Hissing with baby cat claws out one minute, and the next purring in my lap as she was petted. I knew I couldn't get enough of her, and I definitely didn't want our time together to end.

But really, it wouldn't be ending at all if I had my way.

I had a pretty good idea about something else that was going on with me, too.

Like and love are definitely not the same.

I liked to believe I'd experienced both in the course of my life. I did know the difference between the two.

I *did*, didn't I?

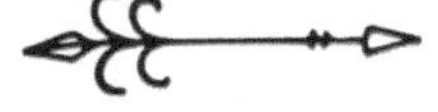

"My friends as promised." Ivan dropped his arms over the fence, brought two fingers up to his lips and delivered a sharp whistle. I figured out who his "friends" were when two white horses lifted their heads from grazing and started making their way toward us immediately. "The one on the left is Silver, and that's Pearl on the right. There's one more friend to meet, but I don't see him with the others. Maybe he'll show up in a minute."

The two white mares continued to come forward, their long, elegant manes and tails being swished by the wind. They were gorgeous beasts, pure white coats with black eyes and muzzles. Just add in a single swirly horn to each forehead and they'd be mythical creatures fit for a fairy tale. "Beautiful... just out of this world beautiful." Nothing else needed to be said. I leaned into the fence and waited for the horses to approach, hoping like hell they would allow me to pet them.

"Indeed," Ivan said softly as he focused on me, looking every inch the aristocratic lord, he'd been born. I still found it strange knowing he was so entrenched in the old aristocracy of England. When I thought of earls and barons, I pictured middle-aged men in tweed jackets and wool caps who cared for nothing beyond the next pheasant shoot. If I caught a glimpse of the House of Lords on television doing their thing in chambers, they appeared in robes with ridiculous collars arguing about something dull nobody cared about, much less understood. Ivan didn't fit my perception of either stereotype. He was young and sexy, and even more so, charming and interesting. There was nothing dull or simple about him. It impressed the heck out of me to know he helped make arguments for important legislation and contributed his expertise as a public servant.

And I'd bet he had no trouble at all looking incredibly hot in his parliamentary robe either. I filed away the image in the secret fantasies portion of my brain. Maybe I could get him to wear it for me sometime. My inner nerd wouldn't know what to do with herself when presented with so much sexy at one time.

I understood his "indeed" wasn't referring to Silver and Pearl as I was. Rather it was a veiled compliment that only served to pull me in deeper with him, into wherever this *thing* between Ivan and me was leading.

He says I'm beautiful.

But he was crazy beautiful for a man.

What in the hell am I doing here with a man like him? Ivan Everley, House of Lords, Baron, Olympian, Greek god, Parliamentary Cabinet Minister to the PM, Romanovs for relatives... and probably more I don't even know about yet.

I was unable to contemplate our situation anymore. My emotions were too taxed to reason out the logic or sensibility of being in an intimate relationship after such a long time of not. I was dreadfully out of practice.

And I'd never been very good to begin with.

"The horses, here in this setting—it is simply incredible, Ivan. I don't think I've ever seen horses so magnificent." I stroked the soft velvet of first Silver and then Pearl, allowing them to smell me before attempting to reach for their necks. I'd been taught that good manners were always appreciated, and animals were no different. Both horses rewarded me with nuzzles, giving me carte blanch to their foreheads so I could rub on them to my heart's content.

Ivan watched.

I knew he was staring again and did my best to ignore him, wondering yet again, why he was so focused on me.

"You know your way around horses, don't you?"

"Yeah, I do," I answered while enjoying the smell of horse up my nose for the first time in a long time. "I love them."

"And you ride?"

"Actually, yes. I took my first riding lesson at four. Over the years, my mother liked to remind me of my announcement after that very first session. Apparently, I informed her that I would be moving into the stables and making the stall into my new bedroom."

"Now that's a scene I have absolutely no trouble imagining," he said, leaning sexily against the fence, his lean muscles showing through the white linen shirt where his arms pulled the fabric tight. "You must have been an independent child, speaking your opinions freely."

"You're probably spot-on there. I am sure my

family would agree with you, there. It's been a while since I've ridden though. I had to leave my horse, Rocket, behind when I moved to London," I said as a dark shape appeared from over the rise and caught my attention. Another horse. A stallion. Pure black and stunningly regal as he came toward us. "Is that the friend you hoped would show up?" I pointed in the stallion's direction.

"Yep. That would be Pontus. Donadea's standing stud, descended from a champion bloodline of racing stock, but he's really just a big lout who earns his keep pleasuring the ladies."

"Ha! Are you sure that's Pontus you're talking about? Could be describing yourself."

He laughed at my analogy and wagged a finger at me. "Your mouth, Miss Hargreave, quite cheeky. I predict some payback will find its way to you... later."

I suppressed the erotic shiver that immediately consumed me and turned my attention toward the approaching Pontus. When Ivan said stuff like that to me, my body responded in ways I'm sure he picked up on. I could only imagine how he might repay me for all my snarky teasing. Pontus distracted the awkward moment by pushing right in between Silver and Pearl and demanding some of the attention.

He nibbled at Ivan's shirt hem and nosed around his hip pocket.

"Yes, mate, I've brought what you want. Finnegan wouldn't let me out of the house without treats for you greedy lot," he murmured. I watched Ivan retrieve a biscuit from his pocket and offer it to Pontus who wasted no time in gobbling it down. "And for you patient beauties as well." He presented one each to Silver and Pearl. The contrast of the mares' dainty acceptance of the treat compared to the messy way in which Pontus demanded his was hilarious. Witnessing Ivan interacting with the horses, and the obvious affection between them racked up even more points with me.

A man who showed his love and affection for animals?

Got me every time.

"So, you're breeding horses here at Donadea."

He nodded. "Polo ponies born here go all over

the world to play. Donadea has been turning out the best in the sport for nearly two centuries. Pontus here is a direct descendant of the original standing stud. A racing champion called Triton who took Haymarket by storm in 1815. After his run through all the racing cups of the day he was moved here from Warwickshire to live out his days and to establish a breeding farm at Donadea. It continues to be a hugely successful enterprise for the estate."

"In Greek mythology Pontus was the god of the sea, father of the fish and other sea creatures, while Triton was styled the messenger of the sea—" I managed to shut off my idiotic rambling and reached out to stroke Pontus, hoping for a distraction from my embarrassment. It helped a little, but not before I felt the flush of heat creep up my neck. I had a habit of spouting off senseless facts that nobody ever cared to know. It was obnoxious.

Ivan moved in to nuzzle the side of my neck where I had to be flushed as red as a beet. "I like it when you talk nerdy to me, Gabrielle, and I'm going to insist we revisit this,"—he placed his hand at my throat; wrapping it around my neck to hold me gently but with the force of something much more binding—"professor-student situation."

I leaned into his nibbling lips. "You do? I was about to apologize for doing the professor routine. I try to refrain, but I can't change the fact that I *am* a gigantic nerd. Anorak, as you Brits say."

"You're right about the Greek names. There have been many aquatic deities named among the horses bred here over the years." He took me by the shoulders and turned me to face him directly. "An educated woman as sexy as you are is a rarity. Don't you know that? It pleases me to see you interested in the world around you. You're an intelligent, passionate, creature with absolutely no reason to apologize for being the gorgeous anorak you are."

He grinned widely, giving me the view of his perfect white teeth but for the space between the middle two. I liked it on him. "Oh, so you agree I'm a nerd?" I pretended to be offended even though I was secretly thrilled about the *gorgeous anorak* remark. "You're supposed to contradict me and say it's not true."

"I would change nothing about you, Gabrielle," he said with a soft shake of his head.

And then, his green eyes grew dark and determined as he leaned in and took my mouth in a blistering kiss that went on for a good while. Plenty long enough to make me forget all about being embarrassed in front of him, or even my own name for that matter. I'd discovered Ivan had a way of making me forget just about everything.

By the time he ended the kiss, I had been reduced to nothing more than a breathless, molten mess. Something Ivan could probably give a class on.

I would change nothing about you, Gabrielle.

It was nice of him to say so, but I was sure that if he knew everything about me, he would never have said it in the first place.

As WE WALKED toward the horse barns, I reached for her hand which she accepted sweetly, curling her delicate fingers around mine in a gentle acknowledgment of trust. Fledgling trust, yes, but she was giving it to *me*. And Christ, did it turn me on to the point of making it bloody difficult to think about anything but having her underneath me again. This woman held power. And she could do some damage with her power if she knew she had it. But I don't think she had any idea at all. She appeared completely unaware of any preconceived judgments regarding me, which made sense really when she didn't have a clue who I was. She'd also been hurt by someone in the past. I'd be lying if I said didn't want to be the one to make that pain disappear. I wanted to help her as much as she could help me. And didn't that just make her all the more unique and alluring?

Fucking irresistible more like.

She enjoyed meeting the other horses and greeted each one separately. I snapped a pic of her with Athena, reminding her that the Greek names for the horses were still in full force after nearly two centuries. She also enjoyed her game of demanding I give her the name of every horse we met. Which I did. Gabrielle enjoyed the hell out of testing me. I don't know why she cared if I knew the names of the horses or not, but it damn well pleased me that she did. I couldn't remember the last time I'd had a guest at Donadea who truly seemed to appreciate the old place as I did.

"So now you've indulged me showing you around the grounds, what part of D.R. do you want to see next?" I asked her the question, even though I knew what she would say. She was itching to get a look at the art. Winding her up was a pleasure all in itself, because soothing her back down again would be my reward... later. *Later* was quickly evolving into something of an obsession. I couldn't get enough alone time with Gabrielle Hargreave, and the realization of that fact had me a tad worried. The feeling of intensity I had when I was with her was like nothing I'd ever felt before. I realized right away I was definitely in uncharted territory, and not completely sure how to proceed. Carefully of course. I would not fuck this up with her a second time.

"D.R.?" She squinted up at me, looking adorably curious.

"Donadea Rothvale is a mouthful. D.R. for short." I looked around at the landscape. "I love it here and it's nice to be able to show it to someone who appreci—"

"Rothvale? You just said *Rothvale*." She jerked her hand, stopping us dead in our tracks as we walked toward the Jeep, her eyes round with surprise.

"Yeees... because Rothvale *is* the baronial title I inherited." What had got her all wound up now?

"Oh, my blessed God, you're *Lord Rothvale*, aren't you!"

She shrieked the accusation at me and stomped her foot, all worked up over something yet again—and ever so lusciously fuckable to me. I wanted to haul her away somewhere for a quick and dirty shag just to take the edge off. I could have those jeans off her in seconds, and the horse barn would do just fine for a bit of privacy—

"I just figured it out," she continued breathily, green eyes still wide. "I—I did not know, Ivan. Nobody ever mentioned your title—just your *name*. Most of the discussion focused on the large amount of uncatalogued paintings you'd inherited, and how you were in need of someone to come over here to take a look in case you had something significant in your collection. Paul Langley had only told me you were a generous patron from an old aristocratic family, and pretty much blackmailed me into accepting the assignment that first time."

"Okay..." I paused, unsure where this line of thought was leading. What did my title have to do with anything? "Well, I've already told you how pleased I am that you've come, I really think there's a bit of fate at work here, don't you? I've so much bloody art. You're a specialist in art. I like—"

"My thesis, Ivan." She pushed her hand on my chest to stop my rambling.

"And your thesis is about?" I really wished she might fill me in at some point because I was not grasping the plot at all.

"Mallerton. My thesis is on Tristan Mallerton, probably the most important Romanticist painter that ever lived. He painted works that were unique and vibrant with life, absent of the dark, stiff, formality that marked the work of artists that came before him. His talent was new and amazing for the period. Innovative. I know you've mentioned to me that you have a Mallerton or two in your collection, but I didn't really have a lot of faith that you knew what you were talking about. Finding Mrs. Gravelle's wedding portrait on your stairwell this morning made me hopeful there might be another undiscovered Mallerton here. And then you told me about the ladies playing cards... and now I find out *you* are freaking Lord Rothvale." She sighed and shook her head back and forth slowly. "I can't believe the irony."

I smiled at her, actually having enjoyed her passionate speech about the genius talent of Mallerton. She could hold her own in a parliamentary pulpit, I would wager, but I still was missing the point of her art history lesson in regard to me. "I still haven't worked out why my being Lord Rothvale is significant, Gabrielle. Don't get me wrong, I am grateful you seem to be so impressed with my title, but I don't ever really use it except formally for parliamentary functions—"

"How long have you been Lord Rothvale,

Ivan?"

"Nearly four years. Why?"

"You really don't know, do you?" She stared at me now, hands on hips, with the breeze moving single strands of her hair in all directions.

"Know what, Gabrielle? What don't I know?" We needed a new topic of conversation, stat. This one was going in useless circles.

"Lord Rothvale number nine is credited for making the career of Tristan Mallerton. He was an early philanthropist for the arts and even one of the original founding members of The National Gallery. He recognized the talent in the young artist and was motivated to nurture that talent by becoming Mallerton's mentor and patron. Lord Rothvale IX and Tristan Mallerton were also very close lifelong friends."

Ahh, the light bulb switched on and even my thick skull allowed in some illumination. If my ancestor was Mallerton's mentor, even I was capable of connecting those dots easily enough. I wasn't that dense. "I knew of the part about Rothvale's involvement in the founding of The National Gallery. My sole reason for having to attend Gallery's charity galas, and, luckily for me, the sole reason I first encountered you, Miss Hargreave." I smiled, remembering how perfect it felt to have her coming apart in my arms.

Gabrielle, however, had more to say, and ignored my dirty reference to our first meeting completely. "Mallerton lived with the family; painting exclusively for Lord Rothvale, who provided a home and a studio so he could focus on his craft with no financial burdens. Without the forward thinking of your Lord Rothvale ancestor, Tristan Mallerton would probably have been lost to the ravages of history because he was born poor. And that would have been an incalculable tragedy."

She gave me a self-satisfied smirk as she finished her second scholarly speech in as many minutes. But I could see how the scale had just dipped in my favor. Significantly. I wouldn't be complaining about it either. If my title was going to help keep Gabrielle at Donadea where I could enjoy her, then the useless thing was finally a fucking bonus for once. *Thank you, Uncle Matthew.* "So, am I to understand that my *Rothvale* legacy art collection just became a bit more of a commodity than you initially thought?"

"Yes! Oh yes, Ivan, there's no telling what you have here at Donadea. I have to see it. Your paintings. Now." She sounded and looked desperate. "Please show me," she begged with a sharp tug to my hand.

"You know, Miss Hargreave, you are incredibly fuckin' sexy when you beg."

"I'll keep that in mind, Lord *Rothvale*," she told me with a backward glance over her shoulder and a devilish little wink, "for *later*." Then she pulled us toward the Willys and flashed me the stunning view that was her arse in some tight jeans.

My cock really appreciated her efforts. I supposed my trip to the gallery with Gabrielle was going to be pleasurably memorable as well. I would make sure she got a full and thorough tour, as a good host should always do.

Chapter 6

The first thing she did after I led her into the gallery was gasp. Then she got quiet as her eyes carefully swept the room as if she didn't want to miss a single thing. "Oh-my-God-Ivan," she covered her mouth with the hand that wasn't clasped in mine, "you have an absolute treasure trove here. There are so many—paintings—paintings everywhere." Then she gently let go of me and stepped farther into the room, immediately beginning to take stock of what was displayed on every wall. "Who is this woman with the greyhound?"

"That would be a former Lady Rothvale with her beloved dog. There's been more Lady Rothvales than Lord Rothvales in the last few generations. Second and even third wives arrived on scene through the years. She's probably the much younger second wife of Lord Rothvale ten if I had to guess."

"So elegant with her coat and hat," Gabrielle said admiringly, scrutinizing the life-sized portrait of a willowy woman in a charcoal silk coat and an enormous hat with lavender flowers, framed by a jeweled-collared black greyhound that matched her clothing as if it'd been planned that way. Probably had been. "I'd place this portrait circa 1910 if I had to guess," she said with a quick nod, repeating my phrasing.

"That sounds about right. It has a very Titanic feel to it, I agree."

"I love that the dog was included in this painting." She sighed as she admired the canvas.

Good. I breathed a small sigh of relief. It didn't take brilliance to see she was pleased with what she'd found here. I tried to explain as much as I knew, which was sadly not much, but I gave it my best. "Dogs do appear in many of the paintings. Most of them are greyhounds, actually. That one over there,"—I pointed to a portrait of a fawn greyhound lying down—"was a special pet because they marked her grave with a carved statue and her name—Zulekia. I can show you on our next walk. I think I remember my uncle saying something about the Rothvale estate in Warwickshire breeding racing dogs at one time. But when I was a boy, and came here to stay, I used to count the animals in the paintings. The people were never as interesting to me as the creatures. And I have to say, animals were depicted a lot, and you see them everywhere in the collection. Dogs, horses, birds, cats, fish, and even one of a little girl with her pet rabbit."

Christ, I was blabbering like a fool, but Gabrielle didn't seem to mind even a tiny bit. She just listened to me as she studied the walls, smiling when she came to something that caught her eye in particular. It all worked in my favor anyway. I could observe and enjoy the pretty view that was Gabrielle Hargreave to my heart's content. And think about how good it would be when I had her underneath me again, all submissive and soft. I was determined not to blow it with her again. I wasn't losing her a third time. "Right. I almost forgot to mention, there are more paintings down in storage beyond what is on display in this room," I told her.

"Aww, I want to see the little girl with the pet rabbit," she commented while continuing to study what was in front of her, proving she could do two things at once. "And you do realize you're taking me down to storage after this, right?" She looked over at me hopefully.

"Yeah, sure." I knew how private it was down in the room where the excess art was stored and felt my cock wake up at the thought. Gabrielle returned her attention to her task, moving from painting to painting without urgency. She was something to watch in action. The scrutiny and attention she gave to each canvas was calculated. I could almost see the cogs turning as she took mental pictures and created a database in her head. "I'm going to leave you to it for a bit. I have some work that needs my attention and now is as good a time as ever. Are you all right in here on your own?"

"Of course." She turned to me and gave up the most beautiful smile, the happiness on her lovely face evident. "Thank you, Ivan—for this—this amazing opportunity. I really just need an hour or two to take some pictures and make some preliminary notes. But I don't even have my phone with me, let alone a camera." She seemed frustrated. Of course she was. Our things hadn't arrived from Hallborough yet.

"Here, use mine and you can send them to yourself when you've got what you need." I handed over my mobile and gave her the code to unlock it. "Feel free to take one of your tits if you get bored with the paintings," I told her with a straight face as I backed toward the door. "I'll be in my study which is on this floor but it's the opposite wing from here if you decide to go exploring," I offered.

"Ahh, that's so very sweet of you, Lord Rothvale, but I can say with confidence that there is absolutely no chance I will get bored with your paintings, so that means equally no chance you'll find any pics of *my tits* on here when you get this back," she said smugly as she held up my mobile, her smirk revealing how much she clearly enjoyed teasing me.

"Ahh, a pity, Miss Hargreave, a tragic pity indeed." I put a fist to my heart, playing along. "Now that you've crushed my hopes, I have no choice but to leave you to your work." I gave her a formal head bow.

She was still laughing at my sincere request for a titty shot when I closed the door behind me, appreciating her sense of humor and wickedly sharp wit. She was the perfect woman, really. She was perfect for *me*.

Gabrielle Hargreave was a beautiful creature inside and out. Intelligent, kind, and genuine. Everything she should be. And by the gods I wanted to keep her. I could only pray it took her a long time to do whatever the hell needed to be done with the paintings here at Donadea.

A very long, fucking time.

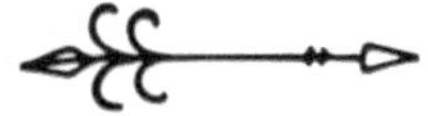

MY EYES COULD BARELY take in what my eyes were privileged enough to be seeing right now. Ladies playing cards, as Ivan had mentioned to me earlier. It was so breathtakingly gorgeous I could do nothing but stare and appreciate it for just the aesthetic value alone. This one was special without a doubt.

It was also another uncatalogued Mallerton, because I could clearly make out his signature at the bottom. That was three Mallerton's so far, if I counted the one at Hallborough, and I'd barely scratched the surface of Donadea's art collection. There was more down in storage, too, according to Ivan. My mind started churning as I replayed all my discoveries today. And it had only been a few hours so far. The sheer quantity of paintings Donadea contained was nearly incomprehensible considering the collection was unknown to the art world. Being in this gallery and seeing the paintings on the walls was like watching a treasure chest being unearthed and broken open after having been buried in a cave for decades.

Ivan, aka Lord Rothvale, was probably the most shocking news I'd gotten. *Ivan Everley is the current Lord Rothvale.* The blood descendant and heir of the man who'd made Tristan Mallerton into the Great Master that he was. This very house had belonged to that other Lord Rothvale, so it was the logical conclusion that Mallerton had likely visited and worked here at Donadea at some point in his life. Mallerton had been very close with Lord and Lady Rothvale IX, considered as one of the family.

But this—this canvas of magnificence before me—was a true gem. I took several photos with Ivan's mobile before opening the *AudioNote* app to record my major observations. My voice sounded giddy even to my ears as I described the painting. Three young women, one blonde and the other two with dark hair, in frothy pale dresses encrusted with bows and yards of delicate silk embellishments sat at a felt card table playing... whist maybe? It was cleverly done too. One of the girls showed her winning hand slyly so the observer could see what she held. Three hearts were displayed along with a knowing expression on her face, the others pleasantly unaware they were about to lose to her.

And the girl showing her hand was indeed one and the same person as Mrs. Gravelle, the bride on the white horse in the painting I'd found this morning decorating the staircase. It made perfect sense that the lovely Mrs. Gravelle had been a relative of Lady Rothvale IX if she was portrayed in at least two separate works of Mallerton on display in this house. The blonde at the card table looked like she could be Lady Rothvale IX from what I could recall from memory. They were all beautiful and young, passing time in one of the approved pursuits for women in their social standing during the era. I wanted to know more about them, their names, their families, how they had lived. Mallerton's work always made you want to know more about the people he had painted.

I really wanted to send a picture of the ladies at cards to Brynne, but I wouldn't. She was off enjoying the start of her honeymoon and I had no business distracting her with work right now. Also, I wasn't ready to disclose exactly where I was or what I was doing there. Because I'd have to explain who I was with, and it would just invite a lot of questions I didn't want to answer right now. Hell, I probably didn't even know the answers to their questions anyway.

What in the world are *you doing here?*

I grimaced at the thought of having to face Ben once I got back to London. He was going to give me hell for sure about Ivan, and I knew he wouldn't let it go until he got some details from me either. That was gonna be fun. *Not.*

So, I made a snap decision. It would be best to gain a better idea of the collection as a whole first, before going public with it. Yes. That made the most logical sense. I roved my eyes longingly over the ladies once more and just enjoyed its beauty for a moment. Utter brilliance and uniquely witty in subject matter, as only Tristan Mallerton could pull off and make it look effortless. People would go nuts when they got a glimpse of this painting. A shiver came over me at the magnitude of just this one discovery. I still couldn't really grasp the entirety of what I was looking at with my own eyes.

A powerful feeling came over my body and held me in place as if my boots were fitted with lead weights. I stood still, unable to take a single step. I could only move my eyes around the room and try to understand the vast collection of priceless works.

Interpretation with paint upon canvas... telling story, after story, after story.

Because every painting had a story. I knew I needed to learn as much as possible about the story each painting had locked inside it. I knew something else too.

More Mallerton's had yet to be revealed.

They were here at Donadea waiting patiently for me to find them.

I knew it with every fiber of my being.

Chapter 7

Gabrielle was still at it when I came back two hours later. The only difference was she'd worked her way to the other side of the room from when I'd left her. "You were right, Ivan," she said dreamily while looking up at the dog painting I'd mentioned to her earlier.

"Of course, I was right," I said, not caring I had no idea at all what she meant. She was pleased and that was good enough for me. I came up behind her and put my hands over her shoulders, unable to keep them to myself a moment longer. She leaned back into me and tilted her head, giving me access in a perfect gesture, letting me know she wanted my touch. It was useless for me to try to resist her, so I didn't even consider it. Instead, I spent the next minute running my lips over the delicious curve of her neck and enjoying her response to my efforts. My curiosity eventually got the better of me though. "What was I right about?"

"The ladies playing cards painting *is* a Mallerton. You know more about your art than you think. And it's not in his catalogue. A new discovery, previously unknown work of Tristan Mallerton just hanging here on your wall."

It pleased me to see her so thrilled with her discoveries. I also felt a great sense of relief a qualified professional was finally here to take on the project. Did I ever expect the qualified professional would be someone like Gabrielle Hargreave?

Ahh—no. Never in a trillion years. I still had moments believing she was really here again and not a figment of my imagination.

That my professional conservator was one in the same as the gorgeous woman I'd been obsessed with ever since the night we'd met in a mistaken identity situation?

Priceless indeed.

"Well, I'm happy you were the one to find it, Gabrielle. I'm sure there'll be more discoveries once you get a chance to see everything."

"Oh, I can only imagine at this point. I've only seen in here so far, but the art is not restricted to just this gallery, it's everywhere all throughout the house, Ivan."

"I know. Imagine having to look at it day after day fully understanding it's being neglected but not doing anything to remedy the situation. That's been an unpleasant weight hanging over my head until now. A true sword of Damocles." I circled my tongue over that spot I loved on her neck, just below her jaw and felt her shiver in response to the touch. Feeling that shiver through my tongue? Downright obscene. But everything Gabrielle did just made me want to touch her, kiss her, or fuck her. "But now, it's your problem to deal with and I feel free." I spoke the truth, even if I neglected to share with her that I also felt like I'd won the National Lottery by buying only a single ticket.

"Well, it's a fine problem to have from my perspective. I could get used to this, you know." She sighed dreamily as she leaned all her weight against me, still facing the art.

"My lips on your neck?" I asked hopefully.

"More like your lips on my neck while I stare at your priceless art collection."

"I can make that happen for you any time you like. This room has locking doors." My mind started running with thoughts of us in here together—fucking wildly amongst the paintings. "Finally putting this room to good use after decades of desertion. I like the way you think, Miss Hargreave, but I'll be honest that I'd hoped you were feeling a bit more hooked than merely 'used to it' by now."

She scoffed. "I am. Oh my God, how could I walk away from all this now that I know it's here? This is beyond anything I could've ever imagined even in my wildest dreams. Your collection—it's incomparable, Ivan, and somehow, by some miracle I've been tasked with uncovering it. Once people find out what you have here, they're going to demand to see it for themselves—"

"No!" I tightened my hold on her. "Nobody else will come," I growled in her ear. Then I turned her around sharply to face me, clutching her shoulders in a tight grip. *You're what's incomparable, my extraordinary beauty.* "I only want you...here," I tried to explain, but knew it wasn't coming out sounding the way I wanted her to hear it. "And *nobody* else will be invited, Gabrielle. Not yet. Maybe not ever. Please understand me when I tell you that I do not allow strangers in my home. Others begin coming here and start poking around in my life? That won't be happening. Never at Donadea—I will not have others fucking about with bloody goddamn everything that's well and good with y—"

I clapped my mouth shut. Turned off the spigot to the word spew that was shocking even to me. I must be out of my mind saying this kind of territorial shit to her. I knew my rant came out a lot harsher than I meant it, but Gabrielle accepted my tirade without any additional commentary.

She couldn't possibly know the real reason I guarded my privacy at Donadea so dearly. It was the only place untainted by the ugliness of my recent past, and barely at that. I meant it to stay untainted. Nothing from the outside was going to penetrate this place and spoil the *only* parts of my life that were good and special. Not ever. Did Gabrielle know she was included in the part that was good and special? Probably not. I doubt she'd believe me, even if I told her. It wasn't the way in which she and I exchanged... yet. I needed time to get us there. Time, I didn't particularly have. I'd have to fight hard for more time with her— keeping my kitten happy and content here with me, away from outside influences. Secrets would be exposed once I was forced to share her with the stupid twats who'd try to take her away from me somehow, some way. I'm fully aware of my first-class arsehole status as a human male. *Flunked out of **Being a Human 101** but aced **Assholery III**.* Gabrielle might've been mocking me when she said it, but she was spot on. And yet, she's giving me a second chance. I don't deserve her, but even so, I'm taking her. Kitten's already mine. She was mine when she fell into my arms at Taunton

Station. Third time's the charm. Fact.

She's mine.

Right, I'm an arrogant prick who does not share well at all. And *I won't be sharing her just yet. The whole sodding world can fuck right off, I only just found her.* I'm not apologizing for feeling this way either—I fucking won't. Been there, done that once before, and it nearly ended me.

But it doesn't have to be the end of the story for me. I know this. I'm not to blame for all the fucked-up shit in my life, even if I realize I'll have to be the one to fix it. I *can* do better. I *want* to do better—for her, *and if I become a better person, maybe there can be an* us?

Expecting blowback from my harshly worded speech, I braced myself for it, but it didn't come. Gabrielle surprised me yet again, as if my rant couldn't faze her in the slightest. *Interesting.*

Instead, she offered me a small tilt of her head before lowering her lovely eyes in deference to my wishes, her submission crystal clear.

The effect of such a lovely gesture raced straight to my cock, by way of my heart. Then the beauteous Miss Gabrielle Hargreave with the green eyes and the mahogany hair, the goddess art specialist from the University of London, the fiery little sexy kitten who needed to be tamed by a master who understood her worth, the extraordinary woman whom fate had dropped directly into my path for a third time, followed it up with an encore. Perfectly wonderful words of her own.

"Agreed. No invitations then. It can be just me for now... *my lord... Rothvale.*"

Words that would seal the deal for me.

Challenge in her green eyes, she was fully aware what the last directive might do to me. *Such a naughty kitten. Making me fall in love with her just little bit more than before.*

I moved my hands from her shoulders where I'd been holding her and slid them up her neck to stop at cupping her cheeks. "Does that mean what I hope it means? An agreement to what I proposed to you earlier?" Bringing both of my thumbs to her neck and pressing them over her pulse points, I was desperate to feel the beat of her heart as she told me something good and wonderful. Just fucking desperate.

Kitten is going to say yes.

Add to that the sight of my hands on her neck? Exquisite.

"Yes, Ivan, it means yes. I've considered it, and I want to be here, and be with you, while I evaluate the Donadea collection. I'll go behind the door and give to you my submission once said door is locked and we are alone together. Which also means no exhibitionism for me. No club scenes either, I won't do that or go to one of those places. I'm a private person and have zero interest in putting on a sex show for anyone other than my partner... ever. If that will work for you, then my answer is yes."

It's been a lifetime since I've felt the need for confession. I'd love to confess to Gabrielle right now, on my knees with a complete unburdening of my many sins. I won't, but I'd fucking love to. Instead, I appreciate what she just told me.

I too, am a private person. Also, it's already been established I don't share well. Imagining anyone else witnessing your submission? To me? Out of the motherfucking question, you silly kitten. Your submission is mine. For my eyes and my pleasure only. And yours too, of course. I already need to kill the cocksucker who hurt you before. Nobody will ever watch us fuck...except me and you.

Fate was surely giving me a shelling. I know I fully deserved it, but this time I was battle ready to meet it head-on. *Bring it. Bring that motherfucking fight on... because I can win it. I want to win this war. Need to, even. It all makes sense now. I know what I want and she's right in front of me.*

This meet-up with destiny finally felt right. Right place. Right time. Right... person.

I studied her in all her divine goddessness, the flavor of her porcelain skin still detectable on my tongue. Her mahogany hair, silky soft beneath fingers possessively laying claim to her elegant neck, for which I had a particular obsession. Green eyes showing me exactly what the manifestation of my destiny would look like if I had my way.

I'll be getting my fucking way.

"Oh, it works, kitten."

Then I took her mouth beneath mine and

thanked her with some kisses. Rough ones and gentle ones, my hands touching wherever the hell I felt like putting them on her beautiful body. I showed her what her answer meant to me by kissing her. To her lips, her neck, her throat, and behind her ear. Needing the intimacy, and yet it couldn't possibly be enough to soothe all the wild desires I had whenever I was with her. Pulling a fistful of her hair back and exposing that gorgeous fucking neck for me to devour, I plundered her mouth with my kisses until I hoped she might understand just how pleased I was with her answer.

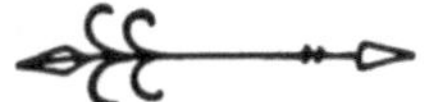

THE VIEW OF Gabrielle's lush arse as she climbed the steps ahead of me, made it damn difficult to keep my hands off it. Doubted I'd last much longer but hoped to get us both safely to the top of the stone stairs before I risked it. The trip down into the catacombs, as I affectionately called it, where more art was held in various states of storage, had been rather uneventful for my beautiful conservator. There wasn't much to see beyond some carved marble statues Gabrielle guessed might be antiquities—not without unboxing crates and crates of God knows what, which wouldn't be happening today in any case.

She announced it was impossible to know what all was down there until every last crate was opened and inventoried. An "enormous undertaking" in her words. All good news as far as I was concerned. Enormous undertakings took a very long time to complete. Just as I'd hoped.

"I'll go down there tomorrow and note the number of crates and their approximate sizes for an estimation in my report, and just leave it there for the moment. You have a ton of art, Ivan. I'll be focusing on what's already on display in the house for now. This project will have to be done one step at a time. I know it sounds ridiculously cliché, but it's the God's honest truth."

"Sometimes cliché is dead-on though, Miss Hargreave. For example, 'lies will get you nowhere, but honesty will get you everywhere.'" I delivered a playful smack to one tight arse cheek and directed her toward the right just as we reached the top of the stairs at ground level.

"You are very handsy, Mr. Everley. Not at all dignified for a lord, now is it?" she purred without turning back. I could feel her glaring at me though, and what was most certainly a smirk on those smart, sassy lips of hers. She was having just as much fun as I was with all the teasing and bantering back and forth, laced with plenty of innuendo.

"I'm the complete opposite of a dignified lord, Miss Hargreave, I assure you."

"Indeed, Mr. Everley, I can believe that." She continued walking ahead of me, never turning around. Since I couldn't see her face, it was fun imagining what her expression might be right at this moment.

"Miss Hargreave, if I might suggest the word *depraved* to be a lot more fitting. Quite honestly, for myself, I find being a depraved lord vastly more appealing than being a dignified lord. Dignified is just so dreadfully boring, and it's really overused, in my opinion. And don't forget that dignified lords are ten a penny in Britain. Depraved lords not so much."

"Hmm... figures." She sniffed, nodding her head as she walked. "Sooo, just to be clear, am I to understand that I'll have to do this important job here at Donadea with a handsy *and* depraved lord for my boss?"

She finally stopped walking and turned, showing me exactly what the expression on her face looked like. Sinful and stunning. Eyes flashing green fire at me and lips far too cheeky for their own good. Most definitely in need of some perfectly applied discipline—while naked.

Fuuuuuuuck.

"Unapologetically handsy and equally depraved, I'm afraid, Miss Hargreave. You will be a very busy *lady*... I foresee." I quirked a brow at her.

She sighed dramatically and crossed her arms over her breasts—a gasping tragedy to be sure—but also an extremely lovely pose on her if I was being truthful. "I'd like to know where you're luring me to now, and for what purpose, Mr. Everley."

This was going to be fun.

"We're coming to it just now." I stepped ahead of her and opened the door to my study, ushering her inside with an arm. "After you, of course, Miss Hargreave."

She stepped inside my study and then proceeded to walk the perimeter, studying the walls and pictures hanging all around her. "Ahh, another room in your house crammed with paintings for me to evaluate. Oh, and it has a door that locks! What an extraordinary coincidence you've brought me to the same sort of place as before, Mr. Everley. I have a question for you. Are there any rooms in your house that *do not* look like this? The kitchen maybe? Or possibly the garden sheds? I didn't see any art hanging on the walls in your garage when you parked your Rover that night in the rain, but then again, I was distracted by being wet and muddy and from arguing with you."

Absolute, fucking, perfection was Gabrielle Hargreave when delivering some well-placed sarcasm. But what if it wasn't sarcasm? Maybe she was having second thoughts because it felt like too much for her to manage. I decided to ask her because I was no longer sure, and I really needed to know. "Are you really complaining about the abundance of art to organize? I can modify your contract—"

She shook her head determinedly. "Not at all, Mr. Everley. Mostly I was curious to know if you brought me in here with the intent to ravish me. Merely asking about any rooms that aren't crammed with art, so I can check them off my list. Are there any?"

I'd love to ravish you, kitten. Again, I couldn't help the laugh that escaped me as I indulged in the verbal sparring with the best of the best. It was fun to talk to someone as interesting and witty as her. "Um... probably, yes? There must be a closet or cupboard that doesn't have any paintings."

"You don't sound at all sure about that." She pursed her lips sexily and snickered at me.

I'm not. This place is a fucking museum. "As much as I'd love to lock the door and drape you over that green chaise over there, and have my *depraved* way with you, I'm afraid it'll have to wait, Miss Hargreave. Not when there's money, contracts, and a non-disclosure still to be sorted. Work must come before pleasure, yes?"

"Oh?" She rolled her lips together and smiled at me. "So, you are a demanding sort of lord then. A real taskmaster when it comes to work?"

I laughed again. "With you, I'm afraid I'll be even more of a taskmaster than usual. I simply have a great deal of work for you to do, and as I've told you before, you'll be very busy day and night."

She nodded her head slowly and said softly, "I figured. The contract better make all of this worth my while then." Then she smiled at me.

"It will, kitten. I'll make sure." I stepped toward her and took her hand. I raised it to my lips and kissed, then tugged her over to the green chaise and indicated that she should sit.

She complied perfectly.

"Actually, I didn't bring you in here to my study to ravish you, although the prospect of doing just that sounds really appealing, I must admit." I winked. "You have that effect on me, Miss Hargreave, every—single—time."

"I know," she said with a devilish little grin.

"I know you know, kitten. You're very perceptive about everything, but enough of that. I have another purpose in bringing you here, despite your very dirty mind, Miss Hargreave, plus I really wanted you to see one of my favorite rooms. This is where I do my work. I think the best view of the estate is from that big window." I nodded toward the floor-to-ceiling window that looked out upon miles of green. Hills and dales dotted with sheep framed by sky and the sea beyond. "I thought you might like an invite into my sanctuary. Nobody else has gotten one of those before—in the four years since it's belonged to me."

"It's a stunning view, Ivan, and I'm honored to be your first guest to receive an invitation. The beauty of this place is unforgettable, and I can clearly see why you call it your sanctuary," she said while studying the view through the window. "Is that a church?" She pointed to the stone chapel and gardens perched into the sloping side of the hill.

"Yeah, that's the chapel. It's not used as a church anymore, and hasn't for decades, but the light is excellent, and it could easily be transformed into a fantastic art studio for painting, or for other any other staging work you may need to do with the collection. I'll show you after we're done here."

"Are you really suggesting your chapel could be my workspace?" she asked incredulously.

"Yes, if you think it'll suit your needs. It's plenty large enough once we clear out benches and such to make room for the easels and tables, or whatever you need. The altar will have to stay though. It's... special, and I don't want to tear it out. I'll show you later and you'll understand." I couldn't wait for her to *understand* why the altar would definitely be staying put. That altar was the pièce de résistance for me and her.

Because I was going to arrange her upon that altar at some point like the decadent feast that she was. And then I was going partake of my lovely feast at the altar de Gabrielle—and by partake I mean fuck—and it would be *something of the marvelous* for both of us.

"Oh my God, there will be no tearing anything out on my account, Ivan. Jesus, don't scare me," she said with wide eyes and a shake of her pretty head. "No altars or any structures are being *torn out* to make room for me to work. Let's just keep things very simple, for me to evaluate and *do no harm* while I'm here. Please?"

Her worry made me want to reassure her, but it would be a lie. *Too late for doing no harm, kitten.* She'd done some... to my heart. Made it vulnerable again. The one part of meeting her I did not care for at all.

She switched the subject smoothly a moment later, probably sensing my change in mood. *Such an intuitive little kitten.* "So, is this where you do your work for Parliament? Tell me you get to pore over secret government dossiers sometimes. Any answers to mysteries from the ages that you can pass along? On the down-low, of course. I promise I won't tell a soul."

"Such as?" I couldn't wait to hear this.

"The Shakespeare authorship question. Who wrote it? The man from Stratford, or the Earl of Oxford under a pseudonym?"

"Look at you, just bursting with the need to know, Miss Hargreave. My money's on the Earl of Oxford." I winked at her. "I'm related to him too."

"Ha! Of course you are, Mr. Everley. You're

related to so many important people, czars included, why not the man who penned Shakespeare?"

Kitten has absolutely no idea how close she is to being pounced on again. "I don't have the definitive answer mind you, but I can get you invited as a special guest to either society, Stratfordian or Oxfordian, and you could ask them yourself. I'm sure any of those stuffy old geezers on either side of the question, would be thrilled to spend an evening sharing their opinions on the matter with someone who looks like you."

She threw her head back and laughed. "No, that's okay. I'm good, Mr. Everley. I'll stick with you." Score one for the American beauty intent upon making me fall in love with her whether I wanted to or not. *You know you want to.*

She patted the chaise with her hand. "You still haven't said why you asked me to come in here if it wasn't to ravish me."

Such a smart, smart mouth you have, kitten. "I thought we could talk about a schedule for being here together." I sat down next to her on the chaise but kept my handsy, depraved hands to myself. I sensed now was a good time for giving Gabrielle a bit of space, even if she wasn't showing it. I'd dropped a whole lot on her shoulders, and she had to be feeling overwhelmed with me right now. It'd be one thing if she were only here to catalogue the collection and nothing else. But I didn't just want her here for the art anymore.

What fucking art? I want her here for me.

I wanted to bring her with me on a kinky fucking adventure of defilement we could play out in private right here without the world having to know. The art was certainly not the driving force for me wanting to keep her at this point, but I was smart enough to know the art was my bargaining chip for keeping her. I'm not that stupid. I also understood what I wanted would complicate things greatly. Kinky fucking came with a pile of complications, unfortunat—

"That's a good idea, actually," she said softly, her attention focused completely on me.

"Sometimes depraved lords just want to talk, Miss Hargreave."

"You're right, of course, Mr. Everley,

apologies for my presumption."

The acquiescence of her words woke my cock right the fuck on up. She was playing with me, of course, but didn't that just feel wonderfully fine? I adjusted my position on the chaise to ease the discomfort of a stiffening prick and explained my situation. "I'm not at Donadea as much as I'd like to be right now. I've come here mostly when Parliament was in recess, until this year with the new cabinet appointment. I've been the whole summer staying at my London townhouse, Brentwood, during the Olympics, so now that's over I've been trying to make up for it by spending as much time at Donadea whenever I possibly can." I walked my fingers over to her hand where she'd elegantly placed it palm down on the chaise. "But now that you, Miss Hargreave, are going to be here working on the collection, I'll want to be here as well,"—I stroked over her hand with my index finger—"with you."

She lifted her eyes from where she'd been watching what I was doing with my fingers, up to meet mine. We stared at each other for a beat. Or maybe it was an hour. Didn't matter, time was irrelevant. We were both thinking about the same filthy things we could be doing to each other. Right? I couldn't think of anything *else* around her. My dick did not possess an off-switch where my kitten was concerned. And not right now either, when her nipples had gotten as hard as my cock was and were calling to me through her pretty green blouse. Who the hell switched on the heat? The room felt blasting hot.

"Yes," she said in a whisper.

Didn't have a clue if her "yes" was a statement or a question, but then again, did it matter? Christ, I was a fucking mess speaking when she was so utterly distracting with her pink lips wet from where she'd just licked over them, and her tits— my God her fucking tits—with their dusky pink nipples budded up tight, all aroused, showing under the emerald green of her blouse, but mostly needing to be under my tongue like an hour ago—

I shook my head once and pulled myself together, hoping what I said next was somewhat coherent. "We need to sort out how this will work logistically for both of us, two people with jobs and school commitments in London, for which there's still three hundred miles and an ocean standing between it and here."

Must've made some sort of sense because she answered me. "I have classes on Tuesdays and Thursdays this term. I could easily be at Donadea on a Friday morning and then stay through Monday night to work on the collection each week. And then I would go back to London on a Tuesday morning. My class doesn't meet until the afternoon on Tuesdays, so I would make it in time easy. I know there are early commuter flights in and out of Belfast—"

"No need for that. I can fly us to London in a blink with Nelly. It's how I commute now. And as it happens, I have to be in London for cabinet meetings on Tuesdays, and for undersecretary meetings on Wednesdays, so this schedule will coordinate well with yours. I could always be called back on other days by the boss, which can't be helped, but I think our schedule couldn't be more perfect really. We can leave early on Tuesday morning and I'll have you in London by nine. Will that work for you this week? It's Sunday now, so that gives us another day before we have to head back to town." *Please say yes, kitten.*

"Yeah, that will work. My schedule's pretty flexible with my commitments in London at the moment actually. I still have my flat I used to share with Brynne, but I do need a new roommate. My dad wants it to be my sister, Danielle. He'd like for her to move to London for good because he thinks she'll be safer here."

"Is she not safe in Santa Barbara?"

Her eyes fluttered down. "She's probably safe, yeah, but our father is a first-class worrier about all things since our mom died three years ago."

"If I had daughters that looked like you, I'd be in a permanent state of barking mad terror. Your father sounds like a sensible man who loves his daughters, to me." *A good father.* Something I wouldn't know from my own, but only through other male relatives who showed me what a good father is supposed to be like. It made me happy to know that Gabrielle and her sister had a father who cared so much. *What did that feel like, I wonder? A caring parent.* I snapped out of my dark musings and remembered something I wanted to tell her. "Since I may need to stay for longer stretches at my London house if the PM requires me, please know you are always welcome to stay over here at Donadea without me in residence. You're free to come and go from here as you wish, any time, Gabrielle. It's a standing invitation."

She laughed softly. "Thank you for that. No more surprises for either of us, right? We don't want a repeat of that crazy night in the rain."

"Ahh, no we do not."

"I get that your privacy means a great deal. I'd want to keep this place a secret too. And I almost forgot that you meet with the PM on the regular, being a member of his cabinet." I still can't believe it. You have a close personal friendship with the prime minister. What other talents do you have, Ivan?"

"I'm not a bad polo player, actually."

She laughed, moving our hands so our positions were reversed. Hers was now covering mine. "Now *that*, is something I need to see." She caressed her thumb softly back and forth over the top of my hand. That she was touching *me* felt fucking nice.

"A polo match?" I asked.

"No, *you* dressed in polo pants and riding boots, carrying a crop. Shirt optional, of course."

Be careful what you wish for, kitten. "Noted, Miss Hargreave," I said, amazed that my voice hadn't cracked when I got the words out. I gave her a curt nod, my mind already going places I'd not dared to go... yet. But if she was suggesting it... So many fantasies to be played out with her. *God.*

She returned my nod with a sultry look and a slow lick of her lips, finishing the whole sexy business off with a scrape of her top teeth over her bottom lip until it popped free. "Mr. Everley, I need to know something."

"What do you need to know, kitten?" My cock was now bone-fucking hard and in possession of every single answer to *anything* Gabrielle ever needed to know right now, in the future, or forever.

"Are you going to ravish me now?"

I didn't bother her with a response.

Chapter 8

One second. And an invitation. That's all it took to turn him.

He transformed from a completely focused mortal man conversing with me on a topic of mutual interest, into a wild, ravening, and very male beast, all in the span of an instant. A beast with an enormous hard cock intent upon putting his enormous, hard cock into me. As quickly as possible.

Oh-kay... if you insist.

I asked for it. And I already knew Ivan could turn it on and off at will. I'd seen him do it over lunch when I'd stupidly assumed a relationship between him and his father. He'd done it at other times since we'd met. I should know him well enough by now. I think I did know. And that's why I teased him. I wanted to turn him just now. *You want him to fuck you, like the wicked kitten you are.*

I did.

And it was worth it. Every kiss to my neck, and each tug on my hair to force an offering of my throat to his mouth was worth it. The rough squeezes to my breasts after he tore my green shirt open were worth it. The little scrape of his teeth when he took a nipple in between and proceeded to softly bite down was so very worth it. The pricking of his beard when he brushed it along my skin—absolutely fucking worth it.

But then he stopped, dropping me down to sprawl on my back on the chaise, tits out from where he pulled my bra up to get at them.

I watched as he stalked over to the door, sharply pulled it closed, and then the snick of a lock being secured. We were alone behind the door. Locked in a room together, private and alone. We both knew what it meant. Each of us had our defined roles now. If I did this with him, then I was cementing the agreement we'd made earlier. To be his submissive. I didn't stand a chance of resisting him the second he turned back toward me and I saw him. His tall and muscled physique, combined with that cut jawline of his, and the dark hair I was obsessed with, all made Ivan Everley into the gorgeous lordly specimen that he was. And right now, for our immediate future in this room together, he would be *my* lord.

He stared me down, his dark hair falling forward from the sharp turn of his head. Combined with the flash of primal green eyes intent upon a sexual conquering made him look even more dangerous than I'd first imagined. Dangerous and dominant as he stalked back over to me, a little gleam of amusement on his lips right before pouncing on me again.

He knelt down and started in undoing the laces of my boots. It took about three seconds for him to get one off and then the other, socks instantly following. "This will be a fast and dirty fuck, kitten, as we don't have a lot of time. I'm assuming you don't mind since you were the one to ask for it. Am I right?"

"Yes, my lord." *Oh, I asked for it all right.*

Ivan was now peeling my jeans down my legs and taking my underwear along with them. "Good little kitten, answering in the correct form. You should get a nice reward for that, I think." As my jeans left me completely and dropped to the floor, I was naked from the waist down, shivering from the way he stared at my body, but also in anticipation of whatever my "reward" might be. "As long as you're quiet." In far less time than he'd done my jeans, he tugged off my shirt, unhooked my bra, and flung both away. "There's to be no screaming, no loud crying, or making a fuss. No matter what I do. You have to be as quiet as a little mouse, even—when—you—come." He took ahold of my chin in one hand and roughly pulled me close, his lips hovering just above mine. "Do you understand the rules?"

"Yes, my lord," I whispered, hoping I'd be able to comply, but also wickedly curious about what he'd do to me if I didn't. The way he was glaring down at me, so aristocratic and imposing, and still fully clothed in contrast to my bare nakedness, had amped me into a state of arousal so intense, I could barely think.

"Clasp your hands together and keep them that way. If I had anything to bind you properly I would." His words were sharp but in no way cruel. This time would be a crash course in instruction—him giving his expectations and how I was to present myself, which up till now he'd never expressed to me. He had bound my hands before, so that wasn't a total surprise, but the silent-play was. If I had to guess, it was because of where we were in his house right now—on the first floor where employees were busy at their work and actively present—and he didn't want his staff to feel uncomfortable knowing what we were doing in his study. A Dom with a conscience, apparently, and it only endeared me more. "Now one last thing before we begin," he said pointedly, eyes darkly roaming all over my very naked and sensitive skin.

I clasped my hands together in front of me, crossing my thumbs into an X to lock them. I lifted my eyes to him and waited.

"You're very fucking perfect right now by the way. That's not my question of course, I just think you need to know how very much you're pleasing me, Miss Hargreave."

His praise shattered the last remaining shreds of reservation I might've still held on to in the darkest corners of my mind. Reservations about whether I should be entering this arrangement with him. They evaporated. Just gone. I *needed* this—whatever we were doing for each other— *needed* it like my next breath.

"Tell me your color, kitten."

"It's green, my lord."

But then he was kissing me again, and I forgot everything else. Since I'd known him, I'd discovered Ivan was a man who liked to kiss. A masterful kisser at that. Ivan never rushed kissing me—before, during, or after the sex, and I now knew I had a serious addiction to his kisses.

To Lord Rothvale's *kisses.*

He kissed me now and I let myself float away, my mind going as silent as my voice. I indulged in the sensation of wonderfulness as I gave over this moment in time to him. He took a little journey with his mouth and plundered mine thoroughly, his tongue pressing inside demandingly hard. When he was good and ready he moved on to work over my neck, making what was certain to be a mark from how hard he sucked on the spot he favored just below where my jaw met my ear. Even though he didn't rush, he was busy as he kissed, a single destination calling to his mouth above all else. My "spectacular tits" as he'd often referred to them. Making a woman feel she is beautiful is a skill that few men possess, but Lord Rothvale was one of them. Lucky me he could make me feel so beautiful when he worshipped over my body like this. Still dressed in his clothes while I was as bare as the day I'd been born, I realized this was how Ivan would fuck me in his study today. He had absolutely no intention of taking off any of his clothes for me in here. I pouted inwardly in disappointment, but it was also a freaking hot trigger at the same time—which I'm sure he knew. Ivan was going to ravish me just as I'd asked him to.

He loomed over me on the green leather chaise and sucked on my nipples slowly, finishing each sucking pull with his teeth in a soft bite until they were tight peaks of sensation. It was hard not to make any vocalization to pleasure. I wanted to, but I wanted to please him more. My breathing sped up when I felt his mouth pull away from a breast to move down my torso. He jerked me down on the chaise to my back simultaneous with opening my legs wide with hard forcing hands. Spread before him, he flared his green eyes for a second before dipping his mouth to my pussy and devouring just as excellently as he'd done to my breasts. I swallowed hard and let my head fall back as the pleasure overtook me and gave in to the orgasm that started building the second his hot tongue began flicking over my clit.

After long minutes of exquisite bliss, when he sensed I was about to come, he stilled his tongue and just blew his hot breath against my pussy, torturing me so damn good I couldn't stop the squeak of protest that came out of my mouth.

"Kitten is not supposed to make sounds, but she just made one." He moved back onto his knees and stared down at me so sternly beautiful, my chest heaving with the pent-up need to come hanging in the air between us. "You deserve some discipline for making that sound, don't you, kitten?"

"Yes, my lord, I—I broke your r-rule," I stammered, trying to meet his gaze *and* to breathe. Which was not an easy feat when he looked so beautifully sexy leering down at me, about to command me to something I desperately wanted to do for him even if I didn't even know what it was yet. I would do whatever he asked, and I'd love doing it.

Ivan jerked me up to sitting again, studying me with fiery eyes as he moved a hand to his jeans, popping the buttons free with ease along with his erection. He stroked his big, long, hard cock in his hand for just a pull or two before saying, "Open your mouth, kitten, because here comes your discipline."

I did.

He buried his cock deep, all the way to the back of my throat where I could feel the tip of him bottoming out. The sides of my head were gripped in his tight hands, totally at his mercy as he worked me on and off his cock with a furious need. I felt my eyes start to water as he fucked my mouth deeply enough to make me gag. He'd let up just long enough for me to take in a breath and then do it again, filling me up just until I reached the point for the involuntary need to expel him from my throat. The extra action as I constricted around his big choking cock deep-throating me is what felt so good.

He told me so.

"Ohhhhhh... you're sooo very good at this." He rumbled out a deep groan of pleasure as he thrust deeply to the back of my throat. "Dealing out cock-sucking discipline to you is definitely my new favorite, but I promised you a fast and dirty fuck and I *always* do what I promise." He held me down on his cock as deep and as far as he could go for a final long moment and then forced my head side to side a few times before releasing me on a low erotic sigh. "What do you have to say about that, kitten?" His hands still gripped both sides of my head as he stared down at me—at what must be my utterly wrecked face wet with tears and saliva from his *discipline*.

He was really asking me if I was still feeling

"green" after being ferociously deep-throated for the last minutes. I understood him completely in all my tear-streaked, naked-skin-tingling glory. "I say yes please, my lord."

Within two seconds he had me on my back again and his cock in me, driving hard, fucking me wildly on the leather chaise in his study—into total, absolute oblivion.

Mine, not his.

I was definitely fucked into oblivion. I couldn't say where he was because he was the one doing the fucking. Even though he could be right there with me on the threshold of Oblivionland, I couldn't *really* know. Either way I didn't have to know. Or do anything other than take it from him. That was *my* role. And it was clear to me that Ivan had perfected *his* role. The sex was so glorious with him. It just worked between us, and it had even from our very first encounter in the storeroom at The National Gallery. Just as he'd said it would be. *How did he know it would be this good?* Being fucked by Ivan Everley was the most perfect sexual experience I'd ever known. For me, in all the ways he dominated me during sex, *he* was simply flawless.

I also loved the soft sounds he made as he let some of his hard-edged control go. My forced silence only heightening every growl and sigh and groan he uttered as he fucked me. And the words he spoke. The way he put his lips on me possessively, and held me in place, and checked in to make sure I was still with him throughout. "Would you like to come, kitten?" he asked roughly.

"Please, my lord, p-please," I sobbed out my answer in a whisper.

"Ahh, I do love it when you beg. So pretty taking my cock without a sound. You're a fucking feast for my eyes, kitten. I'll make you come, but you still have to be quiet, okay?"

I nodded up at him, not trusting myself to even voice my answer at this point. He brought his hand down to find my clit and started working it over with talented fingers in tandem with his pounding cock triggering the magical spot on my body he managed to find every single time he touched me. I rode the wave of the massive orgasm which overtook my body as soon as he added his fingers into the mix. I allowed myself to blissfully crash into a wall of pleasure so powerful I couldn't possibly be whole again after it was over; it was earth shattering.

I barely held on to any awareness of what was happening with him as I came; able only to ride him out to its glorious conclusion. I did sense him getting bigger and harder inside me—how it was even possible I have no idea—right before he commanded me on a harsh rasp, "Open your eyes."

I opened them to the most erotic and carnally beautiful sight of Ivan in the throes of his own orgasm, eyes flared, jaw tightened to a knife-edged sharpness as his cock kicked and jerked inside me. But then, he was no longer filling me up anymore. He'd drawn back to kneel before me, his cock now gripped tightly in his hand. I felt the hot jets hit my body as he came all over my breasts. Targeted placement, of course. He was like a beautiful pagan god of ancient days. Well, he would have looked exactly so if he'd been naked. I was still a tiny bit pouty over the fact he'd kept all his clothes on this time.

As he worked out his cock over me, chest heaving and eyes burning downward, no doubt to view his conquest of me, I tried to sear this image of him into my memory, to keep it with me forever. I didn't want to forget how he looked to me right now in this one moment we'd shared. His handsome face flushed with satisfaction as he came down from the high, his cum marked onto my skin like a brand, the late afternoon sun filtering in around his wide shoulders from the window—

Wait. What in the ever-loving hell is that thing?

Something was hovering outside the large picture window framing Ivan's desk. A dark mechanical object darting up and down, and then side to side with what looked like a lens—oh my fucking God—the *thing* was a drone. And it was watching us.

I screamed.

IVAN'S REACTION WAS INSTANT. He must have read my expression and figured it out because he was up and out the door in about two seconds after my forbidden scream. I could hear the pounding of his feet as he ran down the corridor and away.

I have no idea how I was lucid enough to move myself off the chaise and over to the door, but I did because I locked it again behind him. I then gathered up my clothes, shoving arms and legs into the appropriate openings on autopilot, my eyes on the window which now was thankfully drone-free. I was shaking as I dealt with dressing myself and wiping off what he'd left behind on my chest with tissues from a box on his desk. It was all freaking crazy, but I didn't waste time with the task at hand—first things first. Get myself un-naked and then deal with the situation.

The sight I witnessed happening *outside* as I got dressed from inside held my attention anyway. I couldn't have looked away in any case. It was a truly remarkable scene.

Ivan racing out of the house and over the

grass, his bow drawn with an arrow already notched into place ready to fly. He tracked his target like a hunter, focused and deadly for the object that would meet his arrow. It was strange because I'd never seen him shoot before this moment, but I knew he wouldn't miss. The drone was much higher now, flying away from the house, but the instant he locked all of his finely-honed Olympic skill onto it, that drone was doomed. The arrow he released torpedoed straight for it as if it had a radar tracker, pierced the exterior cleanly, and then dropped the fucking thing to the ground like a stone.

I was witnessing another memory I'd keep and remember of Ivan Everley for as long as I lived. The pure artistry of this man shooting an arrow from his bow was something I didn't want to *ever* forget.

While Ivan was murdering the drone, more people appeared. Mr. Finnegan rushed out with two large greyhounds beside him, one gray and white and one black, and then Marjorie joined along with another tall man I didn't recognize who went over to retrieve the drone. They all gathered around Ivan and had a discussion of sorts. I saw Ivan turn toward the window and gesture something to Mr. Finnegan about me probably, before speaking to the big man who was most likely hired security for the estate. He gave one more glance in my direction before turning away to deal with the unpleasant task of investigating a serious breach of security at his private residence. He looked angry and worried if I had to guess. For a quick minute I thought about going outside as well but decided that wasn't a good idea. Not my place to involve myself in a situation already complicated enough without the added distraction of my presence. Also, the fact I was in no fit state to be *seen* by anyone right now. One look at me and everyone would know what I'd been doing. They might still anyway if images from the drone were recoverable. All Ivan had to do was button up his jeans, which he must've done on the way out while collecting his bow and arrow. I guess it was providence he'd kept his clothes on to fuck me after all.

I understood him a little more than I did before. A celebrity public figure of sorts living in a remote place stacked to the rafters with priceless paintings nobody *should* know about, with his privacy being invaded illegally by someone, and also dangerously in my opinion. He was a sitting cabinet minister so the government might be involved now. I felt badly for him. His reaction to me the first time I showed up to Donadea to surprise him made so much sense now. I wasn't thrilled about the possibility of being recorded having sex with him either. *God.* My sympathies were for Ivan of course, but I couldn't go to that sordid place again in my head. I wouldn't survive the second round of slut-shaming the media would eagerly give me. Hopefully, his destruction of the drone meant something good on that score. We'd have a discussion at some point, but I was confident he'd tell me the truth about our situation. For a guy requiring signed non-disclosure agreements to be around him, he was remarkably open and honest. I *did* trust him.

As he walked out of my sight with his security in tow, I returned to the most critical task of the moment—to pull myself together into enough semblance to leave the study and make my way back upstairs to his bedroom, and more importantly to his marble bathroom where I could indulge in a hot shower or maybe even a bath. I found a small mirror on the wall and dared to take a peek at my reflection.

Not a good look.

My face was a flaming wreck, and my hair was a hot mess, annnnnd I had a large hickey exactly where I thought one might be, just below my ear at my jaw—a place he seemed to favor. Since it was so high on my neck, there was no covering it up with the green shirt I was wearing. More tissues plus water from the *Evian* bottle I found on his desk later, I'd managed to rinse and dry my face. I decided to re-braid my hair to the opposite side to cover the hickey... sort of. The result was as good as it was going to get while being trapped inside the study. I located the trash bin and threw away the tissue evidence, then I put my socks and boots back on.

I went over to the door and put my ear to the edge of the doorframe and listened. Nothing. *Time to make a run for it.*

Unlocking the latch, I cracked the door carefully, prepared to do my very best stealth-walk back to the grand staircase so I could make my escape to the upstairs.

But no such luck was to be had. The two greyhounds were waiting for me on the other side of the door.

I froze, hoping they were only here to make friends with the new girl.

Once I saw warm brown eyes and the slow wag of long tails, I knew I was most likely in danger of being licked more than anything. "Hi guys," I said, crouching down to my knees and holding out my hand. "Who do we have here coming to greet me? I'm Gaby, and I've been invited I promise you."

The gray and white female approached first and licked my hand. She lowered her body down to the floor, that tail of hers wagging fiercely, happy to have me pet her. So very sweet and gentle-mannered. She came closer to my face, and as she did, I was able to read ZULY on her tag. "So that's your name. Zuly. What a pretty name for a pretty girl."

The black one, a male, followed suit and nosed forward to get in on the petting action his sister was receiving. His tag read ZEKE. And while Zeke was a bit more reserved than Zuly, he was still super friendly. He also licked my hand and then sniffed it, but he didn't stop there unfortunately. He kept right on going up my arm to press his snout between my breasts where he stayed, sniffing me deeply. The very same spot where Ivan had presented me with a "pearl necklace" right before the drone incident—oh my God, the dog was smelling the sex on me! *Fuck my life.*

"Yeah, buddy, that's Ivan you smell. It's okay. We're all good friends here." I gave both of them a few more scratches behind the ears before getting to my feet, far past ready to keep my appointment with some hot water and soap in Ivan's bathroom. The dogs followed along after me, seeming determined to escort me. I couldn't stop them—it was their home—so I just went back through the labyrinth of hallways to the staircase where I knew the way to Ivan's bedroom from there. I almost made it, too, but Mr. Finnegan materialized through a doorway at the top of the stairs. Surely I'd been teleported to Hogwarts and here was Professor Dumbledore (just minus the long gray beard) waiting on me.

"Ah, Miss Hargreave, I see you've met the dogs. I hope they've been polite and minded manners with you." If he could pretend everything was normal, then so could I.

"They've been very nice and well behaved. Strange I haven't met them before now though." Mr. Finnegan held out his arm, directing me to follow him, and I wondered where he was taking me.

"Lord Rothvale asked me to keep them separate until he'd had a chance to introduce you," he said as he walked. "These two gave me the slip I'm afraid as I was occupied with—with another matter which required my immediate attention. Apologies for their intrusion, they're very curious creatures, always wanting to be in the thick of things and eager to meet a new friend."

"Zeke and Zuly are lovely dogs, and no apologies are necessary. I was given a very warm welcome downstairs and then they just followed after me as I came upstairs." Mr. Finnegan stopped at a door and opened it, gesturing for me to enter ahead of him. The dogs brought up the rear as the four of us came into the loveliest bedroom done up in pale yellow silks accented with aqua blue and cream. French antique furniture framed a massive bed opposite an arched floor-to-ceiling picture window. As pretty as the décor was, it was the view out the magnificent window that really stole the show. The gardens of Donadea and then the infinity of the ocean beyond. This room looked like a magazine spread in *House Beautiful* or possibly a suite at the Ritz. With a *far* better view than either the one in London or Paris. It was that elegant and sumptuous, but it also felt warm and comfortable at the same time. "What an absolutely gorgeous room," I said in awe as I took in all the prettiness surrounding me. The dogs headed over to a spot of sunlight beaming in through the window onto the lush Aubusson carpet and flopped down to soak up the last bit of warmth before it retreated for the day.

"It's to be yours while you're in residence at Donadea working on the art collection. Lord Rothvale wants you to have this room rather than the one you stayed in the first time you were here." Mr. Finnegan pointed to an open door which led into an adjoining space. "There's a sitting room with a desk for you to work and a place for reading or watching television through there. You'll also find a connecting door into his bedroom on the opposite wall of your sitting room. Your bathroom adjoins this room and your sitting room. I've taken the liberty of moving your formalwear from the Blackstone wedding into the wardrobe here." He pointed to an ornate carved wardrobe fit for a palace before continuing on with his speech. "Lord Rothvale also instructed for you to make yourself at home acquainting yourself with the layout of the house, but he did request you stay inside for the remainder of the day. He also asked specifically you not attempt to leave the estate without him and to please wait for his return, for your safety, of course, Miss Hargreave." He gave me a slight head bow as he finished, his instructions given in that kindly, soft tone I'd come to appreciate.

So, Ivan was worried about me bolting again. Understandable, I guess, but not something he needed to be concerned about on my part. I was fully committed to the job now. "That's no problem. I'll be happy to stay inside and get familiar with my new rooms, which are simply lovely. I'm curious though, did Lord Rothvale leave Donadea?" I wasn't sure what Mr. Finnegan knew about our sexcapades in Ivan's study, but it was clear we both were aware of the security breach by the drone. I reasoned if Ivan *had* left the estate and I was here on my own, it was no different than how it could be later on down the road—I might be working at Donadea someday when Ivan was required to be in London because the PM needed him for government business. Still, I wanted to know the status of my host.

"Yes, he had to go into Belfast to attend to an urgent matter with the police. Lord Rothvale sends his apologies for having to rush away so unexpectedly. He also wanted you to be aware of our security officer, Mr. Sharpe, who is stationed here at the estate, should you meet him at some point today. He may come 'round to check-in and introduce himself later so don't be alarmed by the giant Irishman when you first set eyes on him." Mr. Finnegan raised his hand up to mark how tall Mr. Sharpe must be to tower over his own height, which wasn't slight by any means.

I laughed. "Got it. Giant Irishman is security

officer Mr. Sharpe. I've had a bit of experience recognizing the type over the years, Mr. Finnegan. My father is MetPol, so I've known a few cops in my life," I teased.

"That explains a lot, Miss Hargreave, indeed. Just another reason why you're so well-suited for h—"—he stopped and cleared his throat—"why you're so well suited for taking on the *project* here at Donadea." He gave me another of his signature head bows, snapped his fingers while gesturing at the dogs to exit, and bid me farewell. He then shut the door on his way out and retreated down the hall on nearly silent steps, the clicks of doggy feet making far more sound than his own. Talk about stealth-walking. Mr. Finnegan was a Hogwarts professional.

He also thought I was well-suited for taking on "Lord Rothvale" as he referred to him. I wondered why Ivan was now "Lord Rothvale" when he'd been "Mr. Everley" before. Mr. Finnegan seemed to be playing matchmaker. I'd caught the "you're so well-suited for *him*" he'd tried to cover up by clearing his throat. It made me feel good that Mr. Finnegan approved of me, even though I could sense the lovely old man was up to something behind the scenes.

Very good indeed.

Chapter 9

I'm looking at another Mallerton right now. It's just been hanging on the wall in this lovely sitting room fit for a queen, looking magnificent for the last century or so. Nobody knows it's here, and it's not part of his official body of work. There is no record of its existence, nor is there a date of creation that I've ever seen. This gorgeous portrait of a young woman in a blue riding habit, leading a pale chestnut horse with a newborn lamb in her arms is an unknown. Yet another *unattributed painting of Tristan Mallerton waiting patiently for me to find it in this house.*

Unbelievable...

I knew it as surely as I knew anything about the artist who was the focus of my graduate thesis. It was unsigned, but this painting had been done by Mallerton's talented hand. And I'd bet my life Lady Rothvale IX was the lovely subject of the masterpiece I'd stumbled upon while coming into the sitting room to check it out. I'd seen other paintings of her from among Mallerton's known works. There were a few on display at the Warwickshire estate I'd seen either in person or in photographs. All formal portraits of her in glorious gowns and jewels. There was one special painting of her in a silver gown sitting in a gold chair with her dog resting at her feet. She wore an emerald and pearl choker which could rival anything in the crown jewel collection. It was a well-known work and I'd had a chance to study it closely when it came to the Mallerton Gallery for a cleaning and general inspection a few years ago. I recognized her distinctive dark blonde hair color and the shape of her face. Lady Rothvale IX was a beauty in any century.

I guessed this suite of rooms Mr. Finnegan had assigned to me were none other than the lady's chamber. When he'd said these rooms connected through to Ivan's bedroom it made sense. The lord and lady of the house did not share a bedroom in the old days. They might be nearby in the same wing, but the rooms were separate. Whether the lord and his lady chose to share a bed, and whose bed was used for the sharing was up to them, but each had their own private space dedicated to them for their own use.

Ivan had asked Mr. Finnegan to put me in here specifically; Mr. Finnegan said so when he brought me in. Well now, wasn't this just the bomb.

Certainly wasn't expecting this—*this*—kind of a welcome.

In my defense, it was a lot to take in. I'd only been here a day, and already I'd found so much noteworthy art it was mindboggling for someone like me to comprehend. Because I had the knowledge and training to really *know* what I was looking at. These paintings weren't merely *noteworthy* art anyway. Nope. They were unknown Mallerton masterpieces just resting quietly on the precipice of pushing the fine art world over a cliff into a global frenzy of speculation and interest.

Should any of these paintings come onto the open market or even their very existence publicized, that's exactly what would happen.

I sat down on the comfortable sofa and just took it all in for a few minutes. The décor, the view out the large windows, the details of the painting—the colors, the landscape, and the subjects of horse and beautiful rider so finely worked out onto a piece of canvas over two hundred years ago. And to be looking at an image of the same woman who had lived in this house? In these very rooms which had been her personal private sanctuary, gave me shivers. Ivan's great-great-grandmother. It kind of felt like my destiny to discover all of this. Today Ivan asked me if I believed in fate. Was it fate meeting him the way we met? At an art museum in front of my favorite painting of Mrs. Gravelle on her wedding day?

Yes, I believe it was.

While I was honored to have such a nice place to stay while sorting out his art collection, and beyond blessed to be the lucky conservator to land this job, *nothing* was how I'd imagined it might've been when I'd first come to Donadea. Or meeting

Ivan as his true self—not Mr. Ivanhoe, and certainly not the crazed man who believed I was Maria the escort/spy here to blackmail him with a sex tape. *He is so very different* than either of those personas.

Since he'd brought me to Donadea in his plane, he'd done nothing but make me feel welcome and wanted and... wonderful in a whole lot of ways. The sex was off the chain, yes, but there was more to him than just a handsome man inside a hot body he knew how to use *exceedingly* well. Because Ivan seemed to genuinely like having me in his home. He also seemed obsessed with me being the *only* one to catalogue his collection—to be here at Donadea. Maybe he *was* lonely. I felt that vibe from him when he'd basically begged me to give him the rest of the weekend. He said I was the first woman he'd ever brought to Donadea as his guest. *Lucky, lucky, kitten then.*

Ivan Everley was charming and sexy, yet brutally honest in his behavior and how he chose to live his life. He told me what he wanted and then asked me if I was okay with whatever he demanded. I'd wanted the same, of course, but if

I hadn't been okay, he would have respected my wishes and tried to make sure I felt comfortable. He was a protective and generous person, yet strangely open despite horrific invasions to his privacy. And while his forced invitation to his home might've been a touch unorthodox, I was so very grateful he'd kidnapped me from Ethan and Brynne's wedding to bring me here.

THE BATHROOM attached to my rooms wasn't the modern marble creation that Ivan had in his, but I wasn't disappointed in any way. Its elegance matched the décor of my bedroom in loveliness, but it was the bathtub which was simply magnificent. Four people could probably bathe in it together at the same time if they so desired. My bathroom had also been meticulously renovated at some point and received five glowing stars from me. As soon as I'd done a quick walk-through of my rooms, and sufficiently stared at the painting of Lady Rothvale with the lamb long enough to where I was able to drag my eyes away, I'd fill up that huge tub with a bubble bath worthy of a Hollywood movie and have the most decadent soak of my life.

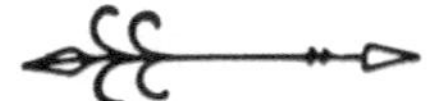

WRAPPED IN A THICK cotton towel, my skin warm from the best bath I could recall in recent memory, I was in need of something to put on my body. My clothing choices were limited until bags arrived from Hallborough, which was hopefully going to be soon. I headed over to the giant wardrobe and opened it up. There on a padded hanger hanging inside the door was the cerulean blue smoking jacket. Almost as if asking, "You rang, my lady?"

Mr. Finnegan took care of all things apparently. My lavender bridesmaid dress and underwear from the wedding was inside, along with my beloved Manolos. Quite literally the sum total of what I'd brought with me—the clothes on my back.

I put on the bra and panties I'd worn at the wedding because they were my only clean option, before donning the blue silk robe I'd become very attached to. Good thing Ivan had given it to me, because I'd already began thinking of it as mine.

I decided the smoking jacket was as "dressed" as I was going to be for the rest of this day and opted for staying in my rooms over exploring the house as Ivan had suggested.

I reasoned that if I went exploring, I'd likely find more Mallertons or similar treasures to freak-out over, and I really needed to slow my roll with that. Seriously. I was desperate to just write down some basic notes on my initial findings—from earlier *today* alone. I was a guest in the private ancestral home of Lord and Lady Rothvale nine for Christ's sake. The same Lord Rothvale who'd made the painting career of Tristan Mallerton. Hell, Mallerton himself had probably stayed here many times and painted glorious pictures, but I didn't feel like treasure-hunting any more for the day. I realized that seemed horribly ungrateful and only slightly less irrational, but I just needed a minute to process and write down some details about the paintings I'd already found today. Tomorrow would be a new day, and I'm sure I'd feel different then. Likely on a crusade to open the crates down in storage to see what hidden treasures I might discover there. Jesus, this was going to be a task.

Hopefully, I wouldn't have to leave the room for a meal, or maybe Ivan would be back soon and have a different plan. But I couldn't waste time worrying about that right now because I'd found pen and paper on the desk in the sitting room. I had a bit of quiet time at my disposal and everything else I needed for writing down observations from what I'd found at Donadea thus far. Once I had access to the internet, I could do more research into exactly when Lord and Lady Rothvale IX had lived here. So, I made a perfect cup of tea for myself, settled in, and got down to work. The next two hours passed in a blink and I did not look up until Mr. Finnegan breezed in announcing he'd come bearing my dinner.

I'd been so absorbed in my notes I hadn't realized the late afternoon had faded into twilight and then into night. Because it was now dark outside. The stars and moon were shining in at me through the window. And *Ivan still wasn't back yet?*

"Mr. Finnegan, you amaze me. Did you

prepare this very delicious meal of roast chicken and potatoes?" I asked him as I enjoyed a bite of buttery mashed potatoes from my plate.

As he'd entered the room with his cart earlier, he'd promptly began setting out a full-course dinner at the small table in front of the window. A table large enough for two, but it would be a table for just one tonight, as Mr. Finnegan had only brought dinner for me apparently. I had wine and everything. This was like room service at the Ritz—probably even nicer than what the Ritz could do.

"Yes indeed, Miss Hargreave, cooking is my enjoyment and I'm always looking to try out new recipes. If you have any particular requests or dietary requirements, please send them along and I'll have a go. Until very recently, there's not been many to cook for at Donadea for the last few years. It's good to be back at work in my kitchen." He smiled at me bigger than I'd ever seen him do thus far, and said, "Might I say that it's a true pleasure having you as a guest here, my dear." He was so sweet. I wanted to give him a huge hug and a kiss on the cheek, but I didn't dare ruin this lovely moment by embarrassing him. I even got an upgrade to "my dear" and everything. *I love Mr. Finnegan.*

"Well, you are a kitchen wizard and I appreciate everything you've prepared since I've been here. It's all been so delicious. Other than a soy allergy I don't have any special dietary requirements. I feel like I'm having a spa weekend or something—and I mean that separate from all the gorgeous art I get to admire as I work."

"Thank you for letting me know about the soy, I'll make a note of it."

I'd be back to my pre-illness weight plus more if I kept eating like this three times a day. "Have you heard from Ivan—I mean, Lord Rothvale? Has he returned to Donadea?"

"Lord Rothvale did check in via his mobile earlier. He sends his apologies, but he had to stay in Belfast longer than anticipated. He did want you to have the documents to read over and sign, however, so I'll be bringing those to you when I return to clear the table. The contracts are printing out now and should be ready for you shortly," he said with a tilt of his head, his hands behind his back."

Well, that answered my question about Ivan. I was on my own here until he returned. "Ah... okay, thank you for the message and also for taking care of me so well, Mr. Finnegan."

He cleared his throat. "Just Finnegan is sufficient whenever you address me, miss."

"Oh... I didn't realize. Will you use Gaby when addressing me?"

He grinned before lowering his eyes to look down at the carpet. "Not a chance, Miss Hargreave."

I smiled back at him. "I didn't think so, *Mr.* Finnegan."

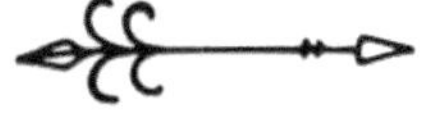

I REALLY WISHED I had my reading glasses right now.

Inspecting important contracts without them wasn't impossible, but it had to be done under a good reading lamp, and slowly, to make sure I was seeing the words as they were written. But if I was reading this CONSULTING AGREEMENT right... a finder's fee of one percent of the sale price of any Donadea-Rothvale artworks sold within the next ten years was due to "Consultant Gabrielle Hargreave of The University of London." In *addition* to a generous monthly stipend for the next year with an extension clause to be negotiated if more time was needed to complete the work after a period of one year had elapsed.

Lord Jesus. I was no numbers expert, but I knew the value of Donadea's art collection had to be in the hundreds of millions of pounds just based on the few paintings I'd been able to identify in a day. There were others I'd only glanced at but knew needed my focused attention. Older works from the seventeenth century looking a whole lot like Dutch masters, and even some Renaissance era paintings here and there on the walls of Donadea. A painting of *Leda and the Swan* had particularly caught my eye. When I first saw it, the hair on the back of my neck stood right up—because it appeared really fucking authentic and eerily... Michelangelo-ish. I'd been too scared to even go there in my mind, because if it were his then I was in way above my pay grade here. Even with the fortune Ivan was paying me. If he had original paintings by Michelangelo, and Pieter Bruegel-the-Elder, and Vermeer in addition to the Mallerton works, the value of his collection would be well over a billion pounds. One percent of a billion was ten million pounds.

Oh. My. God.

That was *if* he sold the paintings. Which from the wording of this contract seemed like his intended goal? Smart, really. Paintings of this value belonged in a museum where they could be secured and shared with the world. The security level here was not sufficient for this collection as it stood. Not even close.

If anyone knew about the art being here at Donadea at all.

But it was especially clear the art world didn't know, though. Hordes of media and speculators would be trying to push their way into Donadea if they *even suspected* it was here. Or attempts to steal it would have been made by now... Rather terrifying to think in either of those scenarios. I needed to tell Ivan in broad strokes what he was sitting on.

Ergo the reason for the non-disclosure agreement, which was all the more important of the two contracts, in my opinion. Nobody could know what I'd found here. Not yet and maybe not for a long time to come. The reason I was here, and the art I had to catalog was going to be on secret squirrel duty. As I read over the NDA further, it covered "any works of historic or artistic value discovered at the Donadea-Rothvale property, the location and contents of aforementioned works to be held in such confidence as to be secret, revealed only with permission from, and at such time of the owner's choosing, Mr. Ivan G. Everley, Lord Rothvale XIII." Further down in the agreement, there was also wordage which covered any private relationship I might undertake with him here or in London, "as exclusive between Gabrielle Hargreave and Ivan Everley, with knowledge of such relationship limited, for security purposes, to family only; friends on individual approval in advance by Ivan Everley."

There would be no contact whatsoever with

the press. "No formal or informal interviews granted to an individual, an affiliated group, or any media organization without the prior approval by both parties." And my favorite bullet statement in the whole thing: "No sharing publicly or otherwise of any knowledge of governmental business of the United Kingdom which might be revealed incidentally due to proximity to cabinet minister, The Secretary of Culture, Olympics, Media and Sport, The Lord Rothvale." So, any government secrets I might overhear from Ivan had to go with me to my grave. *Well, oh-kay then.* Sounded about right for my trip to *Isthisforrealsville* with a layover at *Thisisnotadrill* along the way—just to make sure I got the message loud and clear. Good God.

Of course, absolutely no posting of images or statuses regarding our private relationship to our personal social media accounts. Pretty much anything going on between Ivan and me (professionally or privately) was not to be shared with anyone anywhere. I had no problem with the NDA. In fact, I appreciated every secretive word of it. Ivan was keeping his promise to me that nobody had to know about us. He was a man of his word and I liked that about him, among other things.

I sat back in the chair and looked up to study the room again. This beautiful, elegant suite in an old neo-Gothic manor house set in the remote coastal landscape of Northern Ireland was a literal jewel box.

And the paintings inside it were the jewels.

I was starting to feel sleepy after signing both agreements and leaving them on the desk for Mr. Finnegan to retrieve whenever he reappeared at some point. I think I was just mentally exhausted from all I'd had to take in over the past twenty-four hours. As I leaned back from the desk and yawned, rubbing the top of my head through my hair to soothe my tired, tired brain, I noticed some fancy leather books on a shelf inside the glass cabinet beside the desk. My mind started buzzing because they looked an awful lot like diaries—the sort a lady from the 1800s would use for writing.

I wonder if they belonged to a certain lady who lived here a long time ago. A certain Lady Rothvale perhaps...

My hand was visibly shaking as I opened the door to the cabinet and took a closer look. There were five books all bound the same in red leather. I pulled out the first and held it under the light of the desk lamp to read the gold embossed lettering on the front.

Journal of Lady Imogene Rothvale

The remaining volumes were embossed with the same lettering through to the year 1816. Five years of Lady Rothvale nine's journals were here for me to read?

No effing way.

I opened the book and turned through random pages *carefully* since it was over two hundred years old and saw that each page was literally filled from top to bottom. No wasted space at all. There were a lot of words on these precious pages.

I couldn't read it now though—not without my glasses. I was too tired and too overwhelmed to start in on this discovery tonight, but it was exactly the kind of proof of provenance that would be invaluable if Lady Imogene had written down anything about Tristan Mallerton and the paintings her husband had commissioned in her journals. Almost as valuable as the art itself because her journals would validate the creation of the work in the absence of other recorded documentation of its existence.

I returned the volume carefully to its shelf, switched off the lamp and other lights in the sitting room, and headed into the bedroom to prepare myself for bed and some well-earned sleep.

Once I was under the covers of my sumptuous bed, I saw that I'd forgotten to close the drapes at the big picture window. It was late summer, so the night sky had a glow from the sun on the other side of the planet that didn't happen in California. The night sky here wasn't quite as dark as the southern US states would be, but I was used to it after four years of living in London. The nighttime landscape of Donadea was almost as stunning as the daytime one with the stars and the moon twinkling above the vastness.

I fell asleep while admiring the romantic view of the night sky shining through the picture window from my bed, glad that I hadn't drawn the drapes after all.

And wishing Ivan had returned already, because I had so much to share with him about what I'd discovered.

But I also wanted to tell him that I'd missed him while he'd been gone.

Even as sleepy as I was, I realized I hadn't longed for anyone in the way I was missing Ivan right now.

Never had I ever felt the way I was feeling about him.

Ivan was uniquely special in that way... for me.

Chapter 10

I had every intention of leaving Gabrielle alone to sleep. I truly did. I'd been determined to just go to bed when I returned at nearly half-past eleven.

But shower first. I needed to wash away the day I'd had before sleeping was even possible for me. A day for which the first half had been the best I could remember in forever, and the second half had been utter and complete crap.

My mind was only on her while I was in getting

clean. That she was still here at all was surprisingly remarkable. I hadn't been at all confident it would be the case. But Finnegan assured me she was settled in at her desk hard at work the old-fashioned way—with a pen and paper. He told me the contracts had been delivered for her signature, and to him she'd seemed comfortable and content when he'd left her on her own after clearing away her dinner things. Which was rather unbelievable considering the situation I'd left her in. All afternoon I'd been imagining how she would've demanded a ride to the airport to put as much distance between herself and Donadea (and me) as quickly as possible.

But she didn't. There were no hysterics or pleas to be returned to London. At some point she'd calmly left the study and met the dogs, who fell in love with her immediately according to Finnegan. Then she came back upstairs with them where he'd given her a tour of her new rooms. No surprise about the dogs falling in love with her. Didn't everyone? She had to have seen what I did to that drone though. She was the one to spot it first. Recalling the look on her face when she screamed made me cringe even now. She'd been so perfectly submissive throughout the whole scene in my study—which was so fucking good— until it all went balls up in the worst possible way right at the end. If a single image of us ever saw the light of day, I swear they'll have to add "murderer" to my list of credentials. I was so done with this gross invasion into my privacy. Just completely finished with all of it. If it cost me my job in cabinet, then so be it. I didn't *need* the headache, or the job to live a peaceful life. I had plenty to keep me busy without government responsibilities. Gabrielle would have a lot of questions now, and I'd have to tell her where all this shit came from, and why. I dreaded telling her, but I would because she deserved to know the truth.

Leaving Gabrielle behind today was the hardest thing I'd had to do in a very long time. Leaving her alone, naked and vulnerable as I tried to protect us both from the darkness that tormented my life regularly and now probably hers by association. It was all so tremendously fucked up. Sometimes I just grew weary of wondering what great sin I'd done in my life to make it turn on me this way. The Rothvale curse perhaps?

It was wrong to involve Gabrielle in my problems, but I feared it was too late for that. She was already involved now and my fearing it wouldn't change anything. The minute I'd put her in my plane and brought her into my home she'd become entangled. If she wanted to stick around with me was the question now—and one only she could answer.

Now I'd have to wait until tomorrow morning to find out. Which didn't sit well with me at all in my present state of mind. I wanted to know *now.* Patience can be a raging beast to master. After turning off the water, I just stood there and looked down, letting the water drip off me for a moment. Maybe hoping the chill of the night air on wet skin would temper my need to see her safe in her bed. Just to calm my racing thoughts, which were bloody out of control considering she was just a few doors and a room away from me right now...

Eventually I stepped out and snatched a towel from the heated rack and dried off. I then stalked into my closet and dug around for a while until I found what I was searching for. Another one of those silk robes. What had Gabrielle called it? *A smoking jacket. Fancy robes rich men used to wear for lounging and smoking.* Well, rich was correct, but I'd never smoked anything in my life, and I wasn't going to start. That shit kills. And I didn't need any more help in the killing department. There were some people who'd probably love for me to be dead.

I drew it on and had to admit the cool silk did feel nice against my skin. This smoking jacket wasn't sea blue like the one I'd given to Gabrielle though. It was black and gold and it must have belonged to my uncle? I don't think he ever used it though, because it didn't give the impression of clothing that had been worn. Had Finnegan put it in my closet in the last year or so? It was all just here after the renovations were done to my bedroom. I really had no idea whatsoever where most of the crap in this house came from.

You're rarely here, that's why, you daft idiot.

But I was going to be here a great deal more now. Because Gabrielle would be here. And I wanted to be wherever she was going to be. That was fact. For me, my decision had been made about her the minute she appeared on the railway platform at Taunton Station like a vision from my favorite dream. Fate had given me a third chance with the woman who'd captivated me from the first moment I'd laid eyes on her. And I was done with letting her get away anymore. Because I had plans to win her heart and make her mine. Everyone needs personal goals and Gabrielle was number one on my list.

She's here right now, asleep in the next room.

I looked over at my comfortable bed and thought about getting in it alone. For about two ridiculous seconds.

Fuck that.

I opened the connecting door through to her sitting room and went right on in. I stopped at the desk because I remembered Finnegan saying she'd been working here all evening. I switched on the desk lamp and saw something which helped me gain a bit more confidence for my future—but mostly just to feel fucking aced at the end of a really shit day.

The contracts were signed. *Gabrielle I. Hargreave* had signed her name in a very pretty hand to both. I wanted to know her middle name that began with an *I*. There was so much about

Gabrielle I wanted to know.

So, I switched off the light at the desk and went into her bedroom.

STANDING OVER HER in the dark like a stalkerazzi, I indulged in a little session of sleep watching. I don't know for how long because I was in no hurry. The second my eyes found her, time slowed way down for me and the huge weight crushing in on my chest faded away as if it had never been there. The drapes at the window weren't closed, so the illumination from the summer moon worked to my advantage for appreciating the magnificent vision that was Gabrielle asleep. Even better? Gabrielle asleep in a bed inside *my house.*

She looked amazing in it. Like a goddess in one of the paintings she was here to sort out.

She stirred in the bed and moved the blanket with her arm, exposing one spectacular breast as the covers slipped down. She was sleeping naked in that bed. And I just couldn't hold back my need to touch her for another second longer.

I didn't want to scare her though, so I opted for her hair instead of the bared breast now literally making my mouth water. I caressed a section away from her face to tuck behind her ear, exposing that special place just below her jaw I couldn't keep away from—uh-oh—right where I'd made a damned love bite on her (up till now) perfectly flawless skin. A rather substantial one at that. Kitten's skin was very delicate apparently, and I'd have to be more careful in future. Or maybe I wouldn't. Because having it on her body like a mark claiming her as mine to anyone who saw it there pleased me more than just a little fucking much. The Neanderthal part of my DNA still functioned terribly like that of a primitive male despite eons of human evolution. Couldn't help it. Didn't want to feel any differently than I did about Gabrielle. I always felt like carrying her off to my metaphorical cave and spreading her out naked on my furs for fucking. Every chance I got.

She stirred again. And this time when she stirred, she opened her eyes and spoke to me. She said something so simple. Just three small words.

But the level of intimacy meant more to me than I think anything else she could have said, especially on this night after everything that'd happened today. Right now, in this small space in time for the two of us, the words she said to me meant more than anything I think I'd ever heard from anyone in my whole life.

"I missed you."

She missed me.

She *missed* me.

She missed *me*.

"How did you get to be so fucking perfect? I missed you too, kitten. And this is the only thing which can fix the problem." I ditched the robe and crawled into bed beside her, immediately gathering her against me, loving her reaction of settling right into my arms. I just held her for a moment and breathed in the scent of her, all warm and soft from sleeping. I smelled flowery soap and a hint of maybe citrus in her hair, committing into my memory, learning every small detail I possibly could about this woman who captivated me beyond anything I'd ever experienced before with another person. I *needed* this—being close to her—so badly, and yet didn't even realize until I had her soft skin pressed against mine again just how much I'd needed it. I could feel my emotions leveling out and a sense of calm overtaking my whole body... just from having Gabrielle close again. What did this say about me? *You need her to be* right *in your fucking head.*

"How are you? I worried about you the whole time I was away."

"You did?" She sounded surprised by my declaration.

"Of course. I had to leave you naked and alone while I went out and dealt with a nightmare. I'm so sorry, Gabrielle. I don't even have words for what that was today. I'm just so dreadfully sorry for the many things which went wrong this afternoon. You must think this is a madhouse and me a lunatic in charge of the whole bloody asylum."

"Not today I don't, Mr. Everley." She brought a hand up to tuck my hair behind my ear and kept it there at the side of my face, holding me in place, as she always did whenever she touched me. I couldn't help my reaction to her touch any more than I could stop time. It was simply my reality whenever she put her hands on me. "There was a time when I thought that way about you, but not today," she whispered up at me.

"How's that even possible?" I stared at her in the dark, studying her lovely face and her expression. I almost dared not to breathe as I waited for her response.

"Well, I've gotten to know you since, and today I saw a man doing what he could to protect his property and employees from a threat. You made sure I was taken care of and had everything I needed while you were away. You checked in with Mr. Finnegan and kept me informed of what to do. I was perfectly fine here on my own and found some amazing discoveries that I can't wait to tell you about. I don't think you could kick me out of here now, even if you wanted to. Plus, I signed your contracts, Mr. Everley, so it's a done deal."

God, maybe I had some luck after all. "I spent the first hours imagining you would leave again. Accepting that you might not be here when I got back truly sucked." I found both of her hands and drew them up over her head, pinning her to the bed under me. The need to bind her was overwhelming, but I made do with my hands. She wasn't going anywhere by her own admission. "I hated feeling that way." I kissed the spot on her neck where she had the love bite, swirling over the spot with my tongue, owning the mark I'd made, using the contact to soothe my jagged nerves. "But here you are... and now I need to reassure myself after hours and hours of tortured worrying."

"Here I am." She sighed softly beneath my lips. "So, all of that tortured worrying you did was a waste." She shifted her body against mine, making our lower halves fit together in a way that had my cock banging awake in an instant. Caveman DNA working just as it should. "You don't feel like you're very worried now though," she teased with a little flex of her hips against my hardening cock.

"That's because you're naked and you can't run away without something to cover you. It's a safe bet you're my captive right now, so I'm not too worried at this very moment. When I left you this afternoon, you were naked in my study. And now that I'm back, you're naked in the bed. Do you ever wear any clothes, Miss Hargreave?" I couldn't help chuckling at my own stupid joke.

She thought it was funny apparently though because she laughed right along with me. "When I'm around you, Mr. Everley? Not for long because you're always commanding me to strip. And tonight, I didn't have anything to wear to bed so naked was my only option. It's your fault for abducting me here with only the clothes on my back. What would you have me wear, my lavender chiffon bridesmaid dress?"

"Oh, I think *naked* is your signature look, kitten. You wear it so well. You're soooo fucking sexy in just your silky skin." I skimmed my lips over hers, trailing down her neck to the hollow of her throat, and then even lower to press a soft kiss to the breast I'd wanted to devour since I'd walked in here. But there was more to say before I made her come and got lost inside her. "I absolutely refuse to apologize for abducting you though. In fact, I'm sure bringing you to Donadea was the best decision I've ever made in my life."

She laughed at me and shook her head. "I've

changed my mind, you probably are insane, Mr. Everley."

"Not on that point, I'm not, kitten. Nope. All together in the knob. It's fate that it was you."

"How do you mean?"

"Having you here makes me think you were always meant to be the one to discover my paintings." I nodded for emphasis. "Destiny, kitten—the fates are always at work and I think they did me a good turn with you."

"Yeah, well, I'm feeling pretty lucky to have been offered the job. Fate or not, I'll agree that abducting me *was* a good call. And you did it in such a nice way, Lord Rothvale, so I've forgiven you for your lapse in judgment."

"Perfect." It was the only thing I could think to say before I took her mouth since I was impatient for her now. I longed to kiss her and wipe away the last painful hours I'd endured worrying about her. My sorrows needed drowning in her body, and I wanted to wind her up until she couldn't even think about anything other than my cock buried deep in her cunt as she came all over me. *That* would also be bordering on perfection. I was going to take so much pleasure in giving it to her. And as much as "perfect" seemed too simple a word for the complex creature who was the beauteous Gabrielle Hargreave, it was an absolute fit. The word was the only truthful description that existed for the amazing woman I'd somehow found and now held in my arms.

She *was perfect* in so many ways.

Simply perfect for me.

Chapter 11

My tongue on her clit, and I had her coming against my mouth in about two minutes. Sexiest damn thing to witness her falling apart from the inside out, the way she clawed at the sheets with her hands, her hips raising off the bed, and her back arching as she climaxed. Utterly magnificent. As desperate as I was to be inside her, I wanted her to be ready to take me before I went there. Because I knew I couldn't be gentle. Not tonight, after everything that'd happened. A hard, ruthless fuck is what was needed for the both of us to reset the clock. Her soft, nearly silent, shuddering sighs flipped my switch as she rode the wave of her orgasm—the one thing I demanded from her before she got my cock. Embracing it quietly with a strength of control that defied logic, Gabrielle never broke her composure. Even when things grew intense during sex, she held on to it. So strong willed as she submitted to me. I fucking loved it.

"I have a question I must ask you," I said, crawling up her body, planking over hers.

"What is it?" Her eyes looked glassy, her tits shaking from the heaving breaths she drew in—simply gorgeous in her state of post-orgasmic bliss.

"Is my lady ready to be fucked by her lord?"

"Yes, my lord."

The magic words. Again, something along the lines of fate was at work here. I don't remember ever asking anyone to use the baronial address in the four years it'd been my right to use. Gabrielle was the one exception. Never expected or wanted to hear those words from anybody.

She was the only one I wanted to hear say it.

With her, the words were necessary. I *needed* to hear them because if she used them on me... then it made her... *my lady.*

And now I must show her.

"Good answer, kitten. You always answer correctly though, don't you?" I roughly pushed her legs apart and fitted my aching cock right into place and buried myself all the way to my balls as deep as I could go.

"Ohhhhh," she shuddered the cry as she took me inside, her eyes rolling back for an instant.

"I love this moment with you. Right when we start to fuck." I pounded her hard, the tight squeeze of her cunt pulsing around my cock sending me reeling in a haze of sudden pleasure so powerful I didn't know how long I'd be able to last at this pace. I wanted to last forever. "Remember what I told you the first time I fucked you?" I grated against her ear. "It was true then, and it's still true now."

"Yesssss." She trembled through my hard drilling, her arms above her head, hands clasping desperately for leverage against the headboard. "I know—it—it *is* true—"

She was nearly sobbing as we worked ourselves into a fever together, totally merged in body and spirit. Gabrielle stayed with me the entire way. We fit together so perfectly there was pain mixed with the delirious pleasure. And also, the fear of knowing our connection was something impossible to live without now that I'd found her.

Fucking Gabrielle was painful in a wonderful and a fearsome sort of way for me.

I pulled on her hair and drew her neck back, speaking my words into her ear as I continued fucking into her fiercely. "What did I say to you then, Gabrielle?" I wanted to hear the words come from her lips this time.

"You said, 'I own this body of yours when I have my cock in you.'"

I did own her body in such an intimate moment. Even though I know she gave herself to me freely, I owned her when I was inside her. No doubts there whatsoever. I was dead certain.

"That's right, kitten, and what do you have to

say about it right now?"

Her flashing green eyes, hooded with pleasure, pierced me hard in the heart, just like an arrow might do. Just like my cock was piercing her as I nearly lost my mind from the fucking—it was that good. "I—I'm yours—and I—I belong to you when we... fffuuuuck."

"Yes. You. Do." I started to add sharp twists to my strokes and felt her inner cunt walls gripping me tighter. "And now I want you to come again, kitten. Do it now, just for me, because I told you to."

She served. I could feel the series of spasms start immediately deep within, her inner muscles milking my cock as she tipped over the edge and succumbed. *Fuck, fuck, fuck, yes!* She trembled beneath me and began making the quiet sighs and breaths she made whenever she climaxed. Sounds I loved to hear coming out of her—the ones which made me rise to my own release. Just like that, she came utterly undone in my arms as I speared into her with the moonlight streaming in through the window blanketing us in its unearthly glow.

Thank the gods she did come then, because if

I'd had to hold on a second longer, I would not have been able. I saw her eyes widen as her orgasm detonated, loving that I'd given it to her, and then the splendid climb and resulting collision of my own release as it blasted out of me and into her...

My teeth were nipped in at my favorite spot on her neck, probably making her love bite even bigger, and my cock still spilling the very last of my cum deep inside her when I became aware of what I'd just done.

Oh fuck, I did not *just come inside her without a condom.*

But you did. You fucking just did.

My eyes must've been bulging out of my skull as I adjusted my position and stared down at Gabrielle beneath me. Her eyes were closed but she wore a lovely, well-fucked, blissful expression on her beautiful face just as she should do. Everything seemed normal, but how could that be? My cock was still buried inside her, and I didn't want to leave her yet, but I forced myself to accept what I'd just done to the woman I only wanted to care for and protect. *You fucked her bare and then came in her without asking.* I'd nearly done so this afternoon when we were in my study but had the forethought to pull out in time—at least I think I did. The drone incident happened and distracted me quite honestly. I never got back to discussing the topic with her. Shit fuckery indeed on my part. This was not well done of me at all. We'd never spoken about anything at all regarding safe sex—

"Ahhh, fuck... Gabrielle, I'm so sorry for that just now with no condom. I didn't mean to—I—I'm always safe when I have se—"

I shut off my ridiculous yakking and dared to meet her eyes, now no longer closed, but wide open and looking up at me curiously. "When you have sex with others besides me, you mean?"

"Yessss, but I don't think of you in the same way as others I've been with before, so I don't always remember to use a condom. Christ, I'm really sorry for being so irresponsible and for putting you at risk. But you don't have to worry about catching anything from me. I mean—ah fuck, that sounded bloody awful, didn't it? What I *meant* is that I don't engage in risky sex. I *always* use protection—with everyone but you, apparently—and have a recent test I can show you—with my clean bill of health marked down in black and white. Truly, you don't have anything to worry about there. But what about birth control? Is that going to be a worry at all? I know I'm rambling on and on here, but it's fucking important that you know I didn't mean to do it—"

"It's okay, Ivan. I appreciate your concern, but it's really going to be okay. I believe you when you say you're clean. I'm clean too. And I'm also on birth control. I just had my shot last month, so contraception is covered even if you forget to use a condom. I also haven't been with anyone in well over a year, so my shots have all been precautionary, but every three months I go and get a new one."

"You are an amazing creature, Miss Hargreave, and I really don't know how I can show my appreciation other than this." I leaned in to kiss her and felt her move underneath me, reminding me that our bodies were still very much connected, and that my cock was very happy right where it was. I was also relieved when she returned my kisses, essentially letting me know I hadn't entirely fucked things up with her twice in a single day. By some miracle of holy intervention, I really didn't deserve but accepted anyway, I delivered up my heartfelt thank you to the angel I figured might be helping me out here. *Thank you, Mum, for lookin' out for your son.*

"But I would like to know what you meant by 'not thinking of me in the same way as you think of others' whenever you have sex."

Because nobody even compares to you. "Well, I haven't had any sex like *this* in a long, long time, kitten, if you must know."

"Since you brought it up, I think I must." She winked at me, surprising me yet again. She didn't appear angry or upset either, more like curious in her adorable kittenish sort of way.

"The last time I was with someone was a few days after the gala where I met you at the end of June. I definitely used a condom, and it was a very brief encounter with a paid escort that I can assure you I had no wish to repeat then or after. Her motives for being with me were for the purpose of destroying my reputation at the request of another. In the end, being with her is something I deeply regret for a lot of reasons. I'm not proud of my choices there."

"Okay. I appreciate the honesty, Ivan, but you're not alone either. I've made choices that I'm not proud of. Some of them deeply shameful. It happens to the best of us, but you still haven't told me how I'm different and why I make you forget about practicing safe sex."

"You make me forget my own name, Miss Hargreave, in case you didn't know that already. You are special to me in a way that others are not, and you've managed it in a very short period of time, so just on that alone makes you unique among all women."

She laughed again. Just a sweet, soft laugh that told me everything I needed to know and reaffirmed everything I already knew about her. I'd be keeping her.

"I'm teasing, Ivan. Sometimes you're an easy mark and I can't help myself. But back to the main point of all of this; you need to know that I've been careful, so please don't waste any more time being concerned about knocking me up, okay?"

"Like Ethan and Brynne as soon as they

started shagging?"

"Yeah, exactly like that." She shook her head slowly back and forth. "I don't know how Brynne has kept it together, to be honest. A real shocker for them both—having an unplanned pregnancy drop in their laps within weeks of meeting each other? No, thank you."

"Oh, I think they're both pretty thrilled about the whole thing, actually. I've never known E to be so grounded and dare I say... happy? He'll be a great dad, and I'm sure Brynne will be an amazing mum. They're going to do it all up splendidly."

"I know. You're right, of course, they're so happy and I shouldn't compare myself to Brynne. What I meant was that I'm not ready to be a parent yet. I'm still in school and have career goals to manage. Especially now that I've just landed the best conservation job of the century. For real. I think I'd need to be sedated if I turned up pregnant."

"Why, because you're so young? By the way, how old are you, Miss Hargreave? How badly am I robbing the cradle here? I need to know only so I can add to my ever-expanding list of sins."

She laughed some more and thrust her hips up to make her point that she was still in charge no matter how hard I tried to master her. Again, I was captivated. "I'm twenty-four years young and I just don't feel ready for *that* kind of surprise in my life right now." She pushed on me until I got the hint she wanted me to roll onto my back. Which I did, helping her to settle into position against my side where I could hold on to her more comfortably, even if I had to pull my cock out of her to do it.

"So, how great is my sin if I've got a whole decade on you?" Ten years wasn't too large of an age gap. Was it?

"You're only thirty-four?" She opened her mouth in mock surprise. "That's very young for such an important lord in Parliament. So much younger than I assumed you were." Shaking her head at me as if she were still in disbelief, she smirked and said, "I put you at around forty-five when I first met you—"

I cut off her ridiculous teasing with some much needed tickling until she shrieked a bit more loudly than I think she meant to. I didn't care how much she teased me though, if she was laughing and happy, then bring it on. "Forty-five! Really, kitten, that's a bit harsh, isn't it? Forty-fucking-five my arse."

"Sorry, I couldn't resist, my dear, ancient, Lord Rothvale, you left yourself wide open on that one. I'll probably take advantage of every opening you give me in the future, so best prepare yourself." She looked so beautiful laughing up at me, her long hair spread out wildly on the pillow, the moonlight filtering over her body just enough that I could see her in all her naked splendor. All my mind could process was how good it felt to hear her talking about the future... of us.

"As long as you promise to be here with me, I promise to give you lots and lots of opportunities in future, kitten. Your youthful presence will make me appear younger than I am, and I'll give it my best effort to meet your *every* need and keep you happy, even in my advanced years."

She giggled and placed a kiss upon my cheek. "I think you'll manage just fine if your recent performance is any indication of the stamina your aged body can do."

"That good, huh?" I grinned and raised my

eyebrows at her.

"Have you heard me complaining about your sexual prowess, Lord Rothvale?"

"Not yet, but the night is still young. I could work on it some more just to make sure I've satisfied you thoroughly if you wish." She put a finger to her lips like she was thinking about it, still having far too much fun at my expense for me to let her off the hook entirely. When the opportunity presented, I'd enjoy delivering a well-placed spanking with my hand to her very pretty arse. "Shall I go to my room and get the condoms, so we're prepared this time?"

She shook her head and grinned saucily. "You don't have to use them, I told you already."

"Well, I may be ancient by your standards, but I'm still capable of impregnating you at my great age of thirty-four years. Everything's in working order, Miss Hargreave, I assure you."

"Okay, I'm sensing some insecurity now. Did I do that? I'm sorry if I hurt your feelings with my teasing," she said, making a sad face. "My dear, sexy, Lord Rothvale, does it help for you to know that I think you are extremely hot for thirty-four or otherwise?" She put her hand to my cheek. "Or that I don't think thirty-four is even old? Or that you're the handsomest lord I've ever known—well, you're the only lord I've ever known personally—or seen on television or in a news article? Or that I love how you wear your hair long?" She kissed the edge of my mouth and spoke very close to my lips. "You are nothing like those old lords in Parliament. You can shoot an arrow like a Greek god and you fuck like one too... and you are unbelievably beautiful to me while doing both of those things. You're a man of many talents, but even so, you still won't impregnate me if you don't use a condom."

I rolled her underneath me again and kissed her soundly. Keeping her securely captive until I was good and ready to let her go was something *I* needed after listening to her pretty speech and many compliments. Praise could be tricky, and sometimes it was hard to hear from other people, but hearing it from Gabrielle? Very, very special indeed.

You can shoot an arrow like a Greek god and you fuck like one too... and you are unbelievably beautiful while doing both of those things.

Now that, was something I'd remember for the rest of my days whether my life was long or short. I would see Gabrielle naked in bed beside me telling me she found me unbelievably beautiful when shooting an arrow or when I was fucking her.

There was no better compliment to be had in all the world.

So, when we got down to it a second time, it wasn't the wild, raging fuck of our previous session, but a gentle exploration of our bodies merging together in a way that bordered on a religious experience. At least for me it felt that way. And when I relished the incomparable pleasure of coming inside her without the barrier of a condom between us, I had to think about the consequences of my decision if her birth-control should fail. *We'd be right where Ethan and Brynne are now.*

It didn't stop me from doing it.

I knew I'd do it again if given an opportunity.

Gabrielle pregnant with my child was a rather

wonderful vision to imagine though. Not that I'd try to make it happen under current circumstances. We'd only known each other for a short time, and there was so much still for us to learn about one another before we even got close to taking such a monumental step together. Lots of demons to be put to bed for the both of us I imagined, but if it should happen by accident, I wouldn't be capable of regretting such an experience with her. It would be easier to cut off my own arm than to regret ever finding her, or making a baby together, accidental, or otherwise.

Afterward, when she was snugged into my side and we settled in for what I thought would be to sleep, I sensed she needed to ask me something or wanted to talk more about the events of the day. I kissed the top of her head and inhaled the sweet citrus spice of her hair blended with the scents of our skin and the sex all swirled together. Closing my eyes, I concentrated hard on everything tangible I could frame into my senses so I could tuck this moment away in my memories for safekeeping. Anything at all to help me remember exactly when I knew for certain what was really going on here.

I was falling in love with Gabrielle.

Chapter 12

I almost hated to break the moment between us after the second round of orgasms, but I still had questions. All joking aside about him being ten years older than me, my kinky lord could fuck like a twenty-year-old. On steroids. I didn't like to imagine how he'd honed his skills, but I couldn't help but appreciate the end-result.

His declaration he hadn't been with anyone in the way he was with me "in a long, long time" came as a surprise though. Everyone had their secrets, and Ivan Everley was no exception apparently. We still had a long way to go before we talked about our former relationships with each other. At least I couldn't tell him just yet. I wanted to, but I knew if I told him now, I'd freak myself out and want to go into hiding. My great shame— my part in the destruction of a marriage and a family—and how everything I did now was in atonement for my past sins still had ahold of me emotionally.

I didn't want Ivan to see me as that person.

Or for the knowledge of my sordid story to sour this amazing connection the two of us had found together in the magical land of Donadea, in a castle filled with priceless treasures, hidden away in an enchanted mist where nothing from the outside could break through the magic protecting it. That's truly how I saw myself at Donadea now, and in being with Ivan, too. I couldn't bear for the fairy tale to lose its magical hold over us. Not yet. I wasn't ready to yet face the reality it would all have to come out eventually.

And wasn't that just some straight-up, good old-fashioned denial working on me?

"Ivan?"

"Yes, kitten?"

"Will there be pictures of us on the internet from that drone?"

"I don't think so, but the truthful answer is possibly, yes. I only want to be honest with you so I can't dismiss the possibility entirely. I've never involved the police in this matter until today though. It's in their hands now. Drones have unique registries and can be traced, so if there is a way, the police will be able to find out who or where it came from."

"I—I just need to know whatever you can tell me, please. I am a cop's daughter, after all. I imagine you have some idea just from the way you were all over that thing in an instant, and how you shot it down with a freaking arrow. I watched you from the window and it was quite the show. I knew you'd hit it, too. Before you let your arrow fly, I knew you would take it down."

He sighed heavily and looked over at me, tracing a finger around one side of my face, looking weary to be asked the question, but not unwilling. After a long moment of silent communication between us, he began to talk. And what a story he had to tell...

"Park Jin-ho. A North Korean archer, from a politico family with ties to the Supreme Leader of that country has been my nemesis since we met at the World Archery Championships in Madrid when I was nineteen."

"He competed against you in the Olympics?"

"Oh yes. All three of them. Unfortunately, he didn't get the memo that I'd retired from the sport professionally and was no longer a threat to his fragile ego or mental state or whatever the fuck nonsense is rattling around inside his demented motherfucking head."

"What does he want from you?" I dared to ask.

"The short version is what I'm willing to talk about tonight. Maybe I'll feel differently later, but for now all you need to know is Park has one thing on his mind and it's to discredit me at all costs."

"It's okay, you don't have to tell me if you don't want to. I—I understand it might be too personal or whatever—"

His lips slammed down on mine and shut me up again. His signature lordly move. Ivan kissed me a lot during his conversations with me. I thought it was truly adorable.

"Well, since you're so understanding and kind, I'll tell you he used a tragedy which occurred about six years ago to make it out I was responsible for the deaths of many people, one of them my estranged wife. Yes, I was married for a short time before our union ended quite badly. Divorce proceedings had started and then she died while on holiday with her *lover*. She was five-months pregnant with a child who was not mine, even though her death certificate lists me as the baby's father since we were still legally married. There was a horrific road accident in Italy and seven people were killed. Park used his connections within his family to sell the sordid story to the press concocting a fiction putting me to blame for all those innocent deaths."

I reached out to rub his arm, caressing softly, offering my support. It was all I could think of to do. "Why does Park hate you so much to do something like that to you?"

He clasped my hand rubbing his arm and held on to it. His thumb moved back and forth across the top of my hand in his own gentle caress. "It's just what he does. Tries to take everything from me. He wants all of my happiness and everything good in my life to be taken from me because I was awarded the gold medal, he believed should've gone to him after he was disqualified for an equipment infraction. It happens in professional sports, but he went fucking nutter over the controversial call. After I inherited the Rothvale title and took my place in the House of Lords, he stepped up his stalking game considerably. It seems to get worse with each passing year."

"Oh, Ivan, I'm so sorry. So, you think he sent the drone here to spy on you?"

"Unfortunately, yes. He's done other similar things before. He even rented the townhouse next door to mine in London unbeknownst to me, so he could get video access of who came and went from there. I finally bought it last year when it came up for sale, which is how I discovered his involvement. It never ends. I've gotten death threats that make Ethan certifiably mental having to deal with my security. Thank God he owns a top line security company and knows what the hell he's doing. We were holding our collective breaths throughout the entirety of the Olympics this summer, but nothing ever happened during the games. Probably only due to Ethan's diligence in carrying out security duties. Park has paid an escort to come to my flat to film me on more than one occasion and then leaking those sex tapes to porn sites. There are video clips out there I've had to pay a fortune to get taken down."

"Don't take this the wrong way, because I'm not judging you, but why did you use the escort service if they betrayed you before?"

"The service I used was just the one. The first date was when I met you at the Mallerton Gala. I only arranged for a second date through the service because I really wanted to see you again. I was crushed when it wasn't you who showed up to my door. It was also the final time I was filmed. After, I resigned myself to celibacy and pledged eternal friendship with my hand and a bar of soap in the shower. I'm not kidding."

"Imagining you jerking off in the shower isn't

at all unpleasant to me. Hell, I'd be happy to just hang out and watch you sometime, if it will help."

"Kitten, if you're anywhere remotely in the vicinity of my shower while naked I won't be needing the soap or my hand to get the job done, I can assure you."

"Right. I was just trying to lighten your mood. What about the other times you were recorded then?"

"The other instances it was paid women who weren't posing as escorts at all, but someone I'd meet at an event or cocktail party for work or some other scheduled commitment as if by chance. They were all paid accomplices of Park's though, posing as if they worked for the charity or institution putting on the event. It was a fucked-up shitshow. I learned that Park was following me around via my public schedule, so I stopped having Lowell, my assistant, list it on the website." He looked down at our hands and seemed genuinely bummed. "I'm ashamed of what you might see if you go looking—sexploitation vids going back since I joined the House of Lords."

"I won't go looking on porn sites for videos

of you, Ivan. That's not even in my wheelhouse. Trust me on this, okay?"

"Thank you." He took my hand and kissed it before placing it back down and clasping it again. "Park's fucking demented. He's also breaking the law and I'm going to have him arrested eventually. None of what he's doing is legal. It's only a matter of time until he makes a critical error. The drone registration may help with that. And the fact I've got government security now attached at Donadea. I'd forgone it till now, but starting immediately, I'll have RaSP—that's Royalist and Specialist Protection officers installed at my homes in London and here. I had to let RaSP know what's going on at Donadea with the art, and about you working here indefinitely. On top of everything, I've got to deal with this barking mad lunatic chasing me around trying to do God-knows-fucking-what. Kill me? Burn down my house full of priceless paintings? Jesus, fuck! I'm sort of at the end of my rope with caring at this point. I just want him to stop his fixation with me. I need him removed from my side of the earth."

"Oh my God, no. He cannot know about the art. He's got to be caught and arrested. He can't do this shit to you. Death threats, Ivan? This is just insane what you're telling me."

"He is insane. And I really believe that in the literal sense, which is part of the problem. He's committed a long list of crimes by this point and up till now I'd just dealt with these intrusions via Ethan or on my own. But now, with you here, things are much more complicated. I'm afraid he'll target you with his fuckery—to get to me of course—*if* he knows about you. Which is the main reason I had you sign a non-disclosure before you were in any sort of relationship with me— professional or personal. Do you understand now, Gabrielle, why we need to keep things secret? It's not for my protection, so much as it is for yours. I—I cannot have this touching you. I'll not allow it to happen, again. If Park gets his way and discredits me with another scandal, that'll be the end of things for me."

"What do you mean? What happens if there's another scandal, Ivan?" My panic wasn't really for me so much, but for the hundreds of millions of pounds of art at risk. If this deranged Park Jin-ho gained knowledge of Donadea's priceless collection, which hadn't even been through any valuation yet, he'd try to steal it... or destroy it. *I wouldn't allow that to happen.*

"Well, it's damned inconvenient for the PM to have a sitting cabinet minister with sex tapes on a porn site. I imagine if it materializes this time, I'll no longer be a minister of cabinet. The PM will have to dismiss me whether he wants to or not. I'll return to the House of Lords and life will go on as it did before. I won't work in an official capacity in government anymore; it will be the end of my career in senior politics, I suppose. There'll be no more appointments coming forthwith for Ivan Everley." He shrugged and looked over out the window at the stars. He seemed very frustrated and so dejected, which bothered me more. I did not like seeing him like this.

"So, what will you do if the worst should happen?"

"Same as before. My position in the upper house is secure unless I formally give it up. Being in the House of Lords is not even a paid position. We get an expense account, of course, for our hours served, but it's mostly a public service to

Britain and for me the legacy of my birthright. I do it because I feel it is my duty, but my work there is not necessary for me to be a fulfilled person. I have other work that does pay the bills, so I'd be free to focus more on those ventures."

"The breeding of your world famous polo ponies?"

"Yes, among other things. Donadea is a working farm and attached to the grain fields is the brewery in Belfast which produces the beer. Have you ever heard of Hungry Horse Ale?"

"Hungry Horse is you?" Man, he was involved in so many endeavors. "I love Hungry Horse and order it whenever I see it on the menu. I always ask for it to be served in the bottle because I like looking at the label of the horse with his nose in the hay trough." I smiled at him, hoping it might cheer him up a little.

"I'm honored you like my beer." He picked up my hand again and kissed it once more before going back to staring morosely out the window. I just hated seeing him down. This Park Jin-ho fucker was a true menace and needed removing from the equation by his balls with a large metal hook. If he tried to do harm to any of the paintings at Donadea, I swear he was going to be testicle-free for the remainder of his days. *Crazy fucking asshole.* I wasn't going to just let this go. My dad was a MetPol chief, for fuck's sake. He had to know people who might be able to help with the investigation into what a North Korean national was doing stalking a senior cabinet minister of the British governm—

"The artist who created the label used Pontus as his model," Ivan said with a bit more cheerfulness, interrupting my violent thoughts for the moment.

"I can picture the portrait sitting now. Pontus paying zero attention to the sketch artist while he gobbled away at the treats in his trough." I tried to keep it light, but it was effort on my part.

"Pretty much," he said with a smile before leaning over to give me a soft kiss, his beard stubble scratching against the place below my lips in the most delicious way. "I'll take you there for dinner sometime if you like. There's a restaurant attached to the brewery. And the chef is truly brilliant. It just opened a year ago and took off right from the start, so there's that venture as well as the film production."

"You're a film producer too?" My God, what didn't Ivan do?

"Yes, indeed. Funding mostly, but I got interested when *Game of Thrones* came here to film the show. Before *Game of Thrones*, Northern Ireland was not taken seriously as a screen industry hub in the UK. Now it's taken seriously as a screen industry hub *globally*. It's a burgeoning business and there were opportunities for people like me to get involved, so I did. Anything to help out the local economies where I live. I'd like to be here at Donadea more, so maybe that will become a reality for me now. Point is, I have many irons in the fire. I'll be fine."

"I'm certain you will, Ivan. You're an industrious guy and obviously take great interest in all of your projects. All those businesses sound really interesting and like fun ways to spend your time without the headache of a government job, but you should be able to do what you want without some psycho stalking and tormenting you all the time. The defamation to your character alone has got to be worth a lawsuit or two—"

He shut me up yet again with another deep kiss. I had to admit his method *was* effective. It was impossible to speak when someone's tongue was in your mouth busy licking yours. He was also a really good kisser. I was content to let it go if he was. We needed to sleep at some point tonight.

"Thank you for championing me, kitten. It is very much appreciated, but I need to get off this train for the moment, okay?"

"Sure. We can."

"I just don't want you to run fleeing for the hills, if he starts up more fuckery. As long as you believe I am doing everything I can to protect your work here, as well as your safety when you're in London or with me, then I'm good."

"Then I'm good too. And don't forget about my dad, the MetPol chief. If this Park Jin-ho fucker tries messing with me he's in for a world of hurt and pain he'll *never* see coming. Rob Hargreave has zero tolerance for fuckery of any kind. My dad is a major hardass."

That earned me a full-on laugh from Ivan,

which sounded so good coming from him, it made me laugh too. "I imagine he is, being related to you," he said, seeming much more like himself again. "It must be a family trait because you're a bit of a hardass yourself, Miss Hargreave."

"I hope that's a good thing."

"I told you earlier that I'd change nothing about you, Gabrielle, and I meant it." He took my chin in his hand and spoke very close, his green eyes flashing down at me. "*Nothing* at all."

I nodded up at him, feeling suddenly shy, which made no sense considering everything we'd done and discussed together up to this point. It felt like we'd known each other for years and years instead of just two months.

"Come here and let me hold you." He settled in with me under the covers, tucking me right up against his big body on my side where his arm could support my head. It felt really nice being held by him, and while he was still a stranger in many ways, there wasn't a trace of awkwardness. Yes, we had lots to learn about each other still, but it was the level of solace we seemed to share with each other that made this all feel very familiar and comforting with him. We did *click* as Ivan had told me once. It was almost as if our bodies went through the motions on autopilot, knowing what to say, and what to ask, and when to stay quiet. Where to touch, and when to move, and when to be still. It was weird and yet felt so very normal, like we'd done this a hundred or even a thousand times before. I felt him press his lips to my hair and just keep them there.

"I really am very sorry about today."

"But it wasn't your fault, Ivan."

"Yes, but I still feel terrible about the possibility of us being caught on video. And for not anticipating Park might do something like send in a drone to breach my security. And for leaving you alone while I went out to deal with said drone. You deserved some aftercare, and I wasn't there to give it to you. What if you'd been bound securely by your hands? You would have been left there helpless. I hate that you had to get yourself out of my study all on your own. By the way, how did you manage it?"

"It wasn't that bad. I jumped up and locked the door behind you. I think I got dressed in under a minute while watching you with your bow and arrow through the window. Not even kidding. I cleaned up with tissues and a water bottle from your desk and re-braided my hair using the mirror on the wall. It wasn't my favorite, but it wasn't the worst either. I was fine, honestly. Just felt a teeny bit shocked at first, but only because I didn't know what in the hell was going on yet. I did get to meet your lovely dogs and found this gorgeous lady's chamber bedroom. I even discovered another Mallerton hanging on the wall in my sitting room tonight. It's your great-great-grandmother holding a lamb and leading her horse down the path. So, soooo, beautiful I can hardly bear to look away."

"I know the feeling. But I *will* need to make it up to you very soon for the massive cock-up of today."

"I am very much looking forward to it," I said sleepily, the urge to yawn overwhelming as I tried to stifle it.

"I only want to show you how much it means to me having you here. We have all day tomorrow at Donadea before heading back to London on Tuesday morning. I want it to be a great day for us, so we should go to sleep now and dream all the good dreams."

"I'm so ready to have another great day with you," I said, feeling the immense pull of my eyes to close until I just couldn't keep them open any longer.

But then I heard him whispering sweet words to me in the dark.

"Thank you for being so understanding about *everything* and for signing my contracts, Gabrielle I. Hargreave. What does that *I* stand for, I wonder," he murmured, probably not expecting me to answer.

"India," I said, my eyes still closed.

"Very pretty. It suits you perfectly."

I felt his lips on my hair until I couldn't stay awake for a second longer.

He was kissing me to sleep.

I was being kissed soundly to sleep... by *my* very own Lord Rothvale.

Chapter 13

Gabrielle,

I had to head into Belfast for some quick business with the brewery but will return shortly. Please do some exploring this morning and do ask Finnegan if you need anything at all. Maybe have a look-in at the chapel to see if it will suit for your work needs. Your bags have arrived from Hallborough, so you should have everything you require to dress for riding when I return. I cannot wait to see you on a horse, Miss Hargreave.

Yours,

Ivan xx

P.S. You are stunning in your sleep. I might have snapped a pic or five. All very tasteful though! Hope you aren't too steamed with me. Couldn't help myself—

The note he'd left for me on the pillow was written on heavy cream stationary emblazoned with a heraldic shield and engraved in black traditional font at the top:

Ivan G. Everley
Lord Rothvale XIII
Donadea, County Down, Ulster

I couldn't help studying his writing for any clues he might give me about his personality—about himself. I don't know why, it was just Ivan's own handwriting set down on paper with words of communication for me from him, but it was important to learn it and to know it for some reason. Writing was personal and intimate when carefully put down with ink onto paper. It took time and consideration in a much different way than quickly tapping out a text on a keypad. I traced over the masculine scrawl of his note with my finger. *He took pictures of me when I was sleeping.* The involuntary and extremely erotic shiver that came over me suddenly and with immense power almost felt like a mini orgasm. Imagining Ivan standing over me with a camera taking voyeuristic shots while I slept peacefully in his bed was... quite a wonderful feeling to wake up to. I'd never been left a morning-after note by anyone before. This was one I'd be keeping for my scrapbook.

And hallelujah on the highest, my things had arrived from Hallborough. I now had clothes, my reading glasses, phone, ID, and my wallet. Man, you don't realize how important those few things are until you don't have them. My identity reduced to a bag of essential items. But this was good news. I did have my necessities now, and Ivan was right, I *should* have a look inside the chapel to check it out. He seemed to think it would be a great staging area for the paintings and I couldn't help feeling excited about the idea of having an ancient stone church for an "office." Who wouldn't?

As I headed into the bathroom for a shower, I realized the time was now for me to start making a semblance of a plan on how to tackle my amazing and thrilling new job.

Pinch me, please, because this has got to be a dream, right?

UNPACKING MY SUITCASE was like a little treasure hunt in itself. I hung up my things in the wardrobe and folded the small pieces into the drawers. I'd take my bag back empty to London with me so I could bring more clothes to keep here when we returned next Thursday afternoon. I'd basically be living at Donadea for more days during the week than I would in London, so I'd need more choices than just a weekend's worth of clothes kept here.

Once my clothes were put away, I took my makeup and toiletries case into the bathroom to unpack. It was going to feel so good to have my face on properly again and the tools for styling my hair. But laying innocently on the bottom of my cosmetic tote was something important I'd forgotten about. My antibiotics.

Well, shit. I completely failed to remember

taking them as soon as I arrived at Hallborough. In fact, the last one I'd taken had been at the station right before Ivan picked us up. Over four days ago. I counted pills. Six giant horse pills were still left. This was not good. My doctor at the emergency room had warned me to take them all until the last one was gone or the strep might relapse.

Please, God, no. I took a pill and put another one in my pocket to take in a few hours. I was just gonna have to be optimistic that I wouldn't get sick again.

"GOOD MORNING, Lady Imogene."

Nope, didn't feel weird at all to be speaking to a woman in a painting. She felt like an old friend by now, and so it was only right that I greeted her properly. I'd really come into my sitting room for the purposes of charging my phone, but I simply couldn't pass up the opportunity for admiring the beauty in the painting for a little minute or maybe longer.

I located the outlet beside the desk and plugged in the charger. I braced myself for the explosion of texts that were sure to happen as soon as it powered up in one... two... three—

Yep. Text notifications started pinging like clockwork. Three of them. Hannah, Elaina, and Benny. Of course, Ben had sent me a novel's worth of texts over the past few days so... yeah, I'd have to be careful how I worded my response back to him. He was very intuitive and treated me like a sister, so it was logical he'd be my most difficult challenge in keeping my true reasons for being here a secret. I didn't know how long I'd be able to hold up the charade with him. I'd have to discuss with Ivan in time and maybe we could come up with a solution. Ben was trustworthy and would never put me or anyone at risk, especially if he understood the seriousness of my situation.

The contract I'd signed mentioned family as cleared for knowing, and friends on advance approval by Ivan. Hannah and Ethan were family, so they probably already knew about the art and had maybe even seen it before. Elaina was about to marry Neil, the man in charge at Blackstone Security with Ethan out of the country on his honeymoon for the next three weeks, so there was a good chance Neil was aware of the valuable art and maybe even the drone breach by now. Ethan would know about it too, if he checked in with Ivan anytime in the next week or so, which he'd probably do from his honeymoon. There was no way I'd be able to keep *everything* a secret with this crew. They were already in too deep and too close to Ivan for that to happen.

I decided to send a group text to all three of them for consistency and kept it very brief and light.

Only saying I was having the time of my life enjoying a short weekend in the country for horseback riding and to have a look at Ivan's lovely art collection. That's it. I didn't say there were hundreds of paintings on the walls or mention the wine cellar crammed with sealed crates of contents unknown. I certainly didn't allude to anything intimate between the two of us, or that we'd been going at it nonstop with the sex since I'd arrived. I didn't indicate I was going to be working here for at least the next year, dividing my time between Donadea and London for the foreseeable future. Not today, at least. If they were to be in the know, then Ivan would tell them, and it would be okay. I wasn't going to be the idiot who spilled the beans and put a priceless collection of paintings at great risk.

That person would *not* be me.

I noticed the signed contracts were gone from the desk. They'd been retrieved at some point and probably already on their way to his lawyers for filing.

It's a done deal now. There was no turning back, I decided as I reached inside the glass cabinet and removed Imogene's first journal, dated 1812. With my glasses returned to me, I could now start reading. I couldn't wait to delve into the pages upon pages of her private writings. I had no idea what her words would be like, though. Because individuals had different styles and methods of sharing their thoughts two hundred years ago than they did now. Some journals read like carefully curated lists of the weather, who visited, contents of the mail, and the food served at meals. I hoped Lady Imogene would share things about her life and relationships with her family, but mostly anything at all about the many portraits Tristan Mallerton had painted of her. But I couldn't know for sure I would find such descriptions of the art inside of her journals. They could be five volumes of weather reporting, menus, livestock births, or the egg count gathered per day. It was a crapshoot, and people did have weird obsessions about keeping track of what would seem to be useless information to us today. But then they didn't have an app on a phone or software on a computer to keep their records for them; to know when the last calf was born, or when the baby chicks would be hatching, or when the wheat harvesting should begin, or when to plant the potatoes. People had to write it all down.

I sneaked a peek to the first page with writing on it. It was dated 25th December 1811.

The lovely journals were a gift on Christmas Day from her beloved Graham, and husband-to-be, whom she would marry in one month's time.

I had chills all down my back from reading just the first few lines of Imogene's journal. I had to close it, replacing it carefully back into its spot on the shelf. It was private and special, but that's not why I stopped reading. If I didn't stop now, I wouldn't put it down until the last page had been turned. A read-a-thon was not on my agenda for today. Her journals were going to be a treasure to read. I knew it all the way down in my bones. But they would have to wait for the moment.

Because Ivan was taking me riding, and I was going to spend the day with my kinky Lord Rothvale... having fun together and being happy.

I CHOSE MY JEANS embellished with bohemian silks and the short red jacket I'd brought for the rehearsal dinner for my riding outfit. My brown ankle boots from yesterday, had miraculously been polished and returned to the wardrobe at some point. Mr. Finnegan was a stealth master indeed. Like, when did he come in here and do these things? Hopefully, he had some help below who did the actual laundry. I didn't like to think of him slaving away on my behalf, washing my clothes and shining my boots at his age. He should be allowed to do the things he loved, like making those delicious scones.

I was pretty sure I could smell them baking actually as I followed my nose to the kitchen. I was greeted by Zeke and Zuly just as Mr. Finnegan was removing a pan of them from the ovens.

"Ahh, I thought I smelled your delicious scones, Mr. Finnegan. My nose led me straight here with no problem."

"I was anticipating you, Miss Hargreave. I am determined to feed you my scones straight out of the oven, and I won't take no for an answer this time." He smiled at me and indicated with his head. "I have your tea ready at the counter, if you'd like to eat in here with me you are most welcome."

I was being invited to eat breakfast in Mr. Finnegan's kitchen?

"And I am going to say 'yes please' to your offer, Mr. Finnegan. No need to twist my arm today." I gave the dogs some attention first and then made my way over to the counter and sat on a modern high-backed stool. The kitchen was huge and had been through a recent renovation.

The only clue as to the true age of the house in this room was the great fireplace that had probably once been used for cooking entire animals within it. Now it was just a warm place for the dogs to have their beds beside a cozy fire when the weather grew cold.

I asked him questions about the house, and he asked me about my studies in London as he stirred away at something spicy in a pot. It was comfortable and easy talking to him, and I would be spending a lot of time in his company in the next year, so it made sense now to get to know each other better.

When paired with the Irish butter and the raspberry jam, Mr. Finnegan's scones bordered on something of a sacred experience. I told him so as I finished the last decadent bite from my plate. Mr. Finnegan thanked me kindly for the compliment and then took a seat on the stool next to me. It was a surprise, because I'd never seen him sit before. He was always busy doing something where you never quite witnessed the process, only the end result.

"How long have you been here at Donadea,

Mr. Finnegan?" I asked cautiously, not quite sure what he was up to.

"Since I was a boy of twelve and my mother came here to be the cook for Lord Rothvale's grandfather, number eleven. I have served at Donadea for over fifty years now. It's really the only home I've ever known."

"It must have changed a great deal in fifty years, but it's still an amazing and beautiful house in the most gorgeous setting. I can't imagine a better place to be if you are a lover of country living."

"Very true, and it's coming into a kind of Renaissance now that number thirteen has taken such a keen interest in the place. He is working hard to make it a comfortable home once more after some years of neglect."

"You call him number thirteen?" I suppose it made sense to keep track of who was who among the staff.

"Not to his face of course. Usually 'sir' works well for most situations. He doesn't care for formalities much, but it's not easy for an old dog like me to learn new tricks, either."

I grinned conspiratorially. "He told me when you use the baronial address it's because you're annoyed with him." It wasn't quite the whole truth, but close enough to get the general meaning across. I would *not* be sharing with him what Ivan had really said. *When he uses my lord on me, Finnegan is undoubtedly telling me to fuck off.*

"Did he now? I'll make a note. Might come in handy in future, you never know." He smiled gently and looked me straight in the eyes. "If I may, I'd like to share something with you, Miss Hargreave, about... him. I'd also ask for your confidence in keeping this between us if you would. He would not be pleased with me for sharing the details about his past, but I'm going to go out on a limb here because I believe I can trust you. And I know you'll now be a fixture here at Donadea as you work with the paintings."

Okay, my ears were now tuned in a million percent to Mr. Finnegan and what he might tell me. "Of course, you can trust me. I'm only here to help him, Mr. Finnegan."

"I'd venture it's a bit more than that though,

between the two of you, Miss Hargreave. And it is for that reason, I'm talking to you now. I've known him since the day he was born when his mother brought him home wrapped in a white lambswool blanket. He was born at the hospital in Belfast and lived here with her until she was lost to him at the age of six. He was shuttled between his grandmothers and his uncle mostly for the next few years until he was old enough to be sent off to the exclusive schools for young men of his status, as is the custom."

"Where was his father?" I dared to ask.

"Absent is the best answer I can give you. His father grew disinterested in family life shortly after Ivan was born and divorced himself from his wife and son well before Ivan's first birthday. His uncle Matthew, Lord Rothvale number twelve, invited Rebecca, Ivan's mother, to live here at Donadea for as long as she wished, and she did. She made Donadea their home while Ivan's father lived in various places in Europe and in London. Ivan did not meet his father in person for the first time until well after his mother had died. Matthew never married or had any children, so Ivan was *his* heir.

For all intents and purposes, Matthew Everley was the only *father* that boy ever knew. Matthew did the best he could with him. And that is how Ivan came to be number thirteen when Matthew died four years ago after a short bout with cancer."

"This is a very sad story you've just told me, Mr. Finnegan. I—I can't imagine him growing up without parents to love him." The thought of little Ivan basically an orphan at six years old just wrecked me to the point of wanting to crawl into a corner and sob.

He smiled at me again and reached out to clasp my hand. "This is why I wanted you to understand the road he's traveled throughout his life has been a lonely one. He's had a very privileged upbringing, but one rather lacking in love and affection from people who were either not present in his life or left this world far too soon. He's had to be on his own at a young age when there was nobody to guide him or give support. I know he's not easy all the time. He can be exacting, and demanding, and at times, temperamental. I do realize he has his flaws just as we all do, but if I may say, you seem able to manage him quite effortlessly, but more importantly, you are making him happy. I have never known him to be so lighthearted in all the years before you arrived on scene, Miss Hargreave. It's you. You've made this sudden change in him, and if I might be so bold in saying this next part, it's because he cares a great deal for you. I do know that to be true."

"I care about him, too. So much. He makes *me* happy, and he's a very special person to me even without his amazing collection of art. I think I understand him better now, so thank you for sharing the context of his early life with me. I won't say anything to him. This conversation never happened, but I am going to need a hug now, Mr. Finnegan, because that's just how I roll when I'm feeling like I might cry."

As Mr. Finnegan held me and patted me on the back, the warmth of his embrace made me feel better, and also very grateful Ivan at least had *someone* who cared looking out for him over the years. He might not have said the actual words, but Mr. Finnegan loved Ivan like a son. He did love him. He never would've told me about Ivan's heartbreaking childhood if he didn't.

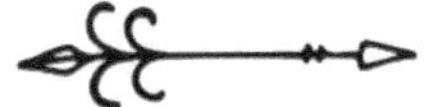

I NEEDED A LITTLE quiet reflection in a church after the emotional conversation with Mr. Finnegan over tea and scones in the kitchen. The chapel felt like the best place to stop next on my whirlwind tour. I wasn't left completely on my own though. Zeke and Zuly were determined to be attached to me whether I desired company or not. I think they sensed my melancholy after hearing about Ivan's childhood and wanted to comfort me. Pets were intuitive when their humans felt sad. It was rough just listening to Mr. Finnegan tell it. Imagining Ivan having to live it was far worse. How he'd come through such a heartbreaking early life to become the charming and generous guy with the easy-going personality was quite the mystery. Add to that the disaster of his first marriage and his wife's death—Ivan's life read a lot like a Shakespearean tragedy.

I opened the heavy wooden door shaped in a Gothic arch and stepped inside with the dogs right behind me.

And fell instantly in love with the space.

So much light poured in through the many Gothic windows of clear glass above and stained glass mosaics at the lowest levels. I could see what he meant about the altar and not wanting to remove it. It was a gorgeous carved wooden masterpiece with animals and scenes from nature carved into all four panels. There was no way for it to be moved without destroying it, so stay it must.

A curious painting of an angel caught my eye on the wall behind the altar. As I came closer to study it more carefully, I could see it was of a woman who looked a whole lot like Imogene in a white robe with wings pointed upward as if she were ascending to the heavens. Two small doves above her right shoulder flew with her. The whole thing had a William Blake quality to it, ethereal but also peaceful, evoking a sense of serenity and comforting calmness. I reached for my glasses in my jacket pocket and put them on. I found the artists' mark in the bottom right quadrant:

B.E. Russell
"Mamma" –1876

It took me a moment, but I figured it out. Byrony Everley Russell, daughter of Lord and Lady Rothvale number nine, was an accomplished artist in her own lifetime, well-known for her more mystical style rather than romanticist, but still hugely popular with collectors today. This was a simply gorgeous example of her work, even though it needed a thorough cleaning after nearly one hundred and fifty years of living in a chapel where candles were burned perpetually during the days when it was in use.

A Byrony Everley Russell just hanging on a wall for the last century and a half, in the old stone church I'd be using as a staging area for my work at Donadea.

Unbelievable.

The date of 1876 made this canvas a lot more recent than any of the Mallerton portraits of Imogene, so the daughter portrayed her mother as a much younger woman than she would've been in 1876... which meant this was done by Byrony to memorialize her mother after Imogene's death. As an angel or as a living woman, I had to agree putting her in the chapel did seem like the most appropriate place for a beautiful angel to repose...

I took out my phone and snapped some pictures. If Ivan sold the Russell to a private collector, he could get a million pounds or more for this one portrait alone. Her work was very much in demand.

In fact, Ivan would have no problem selling off any of the paintings he wished to move. I agreed with him. There was far too much stored in one place. A fire could wipe everything out in mere minutes, and then it would all be lost forever—an incalculable loss for the art world.

And putting irreplaceable paintings such as this at risk was simply not an option.

Chapter 14

When I saw her bending down studying something on the ground what looked like it could be wildflowers, I just couldn't help myself. I'd been impatiently waiting on her and was about to start out searching when I spotted her red jacket across the field from the horse barns. The dogs were with her, just as they should be when the mistress was outside walking on her own. After the incident with the drone yesterday, I wouldn't be taking any chances with her protection, either here or in London. If

Park Jin-ho targeted Gabrielle for any sort of abuse or threats to frighten her or otherwise, I'd fucking lose my mind. I'd be the one in need of a white coat with extra-long arms and a padded cell instead of him.

The guard dog army would be here in another month. Arriving direct from Prague with a handler who would live with them on the property and keep the undesirables out. Trained working security animals who did not fuck around and attacked on demand when trespassed upon. Posted warning signs >>GUARD DOGS ON PREMISES - DO NOT ENTER<< would be going up soon across the entirety of the lands of this estate. It was Ethan's suggestion actually, and I was fully on board with the idea now.

But at this very moment my thoughts were being distracted by the vision of Gabrielle's luscious bum in another pair of tight jeans, these with many colorful silk patches on them, bent over to admire the purple flowers blooming profusely in the fields this time of the year. I pushed Pontus forward and hoped the noise of the breeze blowing away from her would muffle the sound of his steps.

PRETTY LAVENDER FLOWERS bloomed all over the ground in clumps, but they weren't the species *lavender* though, they were more like thistle flowers sans the prickles. I was in awe of the beauty of this place. Donadea was filled with treasures inside the house, yes, but many natural treasures existed on the land of the estate, too. No wonder Ivan loved it here so much. He was born here, and his first memories of life were here. Donadea was as special as the people who had made it their home and lived their lives here for centuries. It was as special as Ivan Everley had become to me. I understood so much more about him than before. Everything about him made sense to me now. Why he was a dominant and so protective of his privacy and the ones he loved.

The ones he loved...

Did he love me? Mr. Finnegan seemed to

think so, even if he didn't frame it in those exact words. Ivan was honest though, if he felt a certain way, he would probably not be shy about saying it. I knew he wanted me here. He'd told me many, many times by now. He also said it again last night as he was kissing me to sleep. The ultimate in swoony moments of all tim—

A hard, blunt nudge from something big poked me right in the ass!

"Ooooh!" I squeaked just before I heard the deep laughter I'd come to know quite well by now, coming from... above me? I whipped my head around so fast my hair hit me on the other side of my cheek, only to find Ivan sitting on top of Pontus in riding clothes and wearing tall leather boots.

"Sorry, kitten, it was too perfect an opportunity to pass up, and you were so very focused on admiring those little flowers, you never heard us coming."

"Uh-huh, a likely story," I said, shielding the sun from my eyes with my hand as I looked up and studied him. The man could sit a horse well. And those tall riding boots... and his long hair... and the riding pants. Was he wearing his polo uniform? I felt my mouth start to water, and I swallowed deeply before reaching out to stroke Pontus from his long black forehead down to his muzzle. "That wasn't very gentlemanly of you, Pontus, but I don't blame you, sir. Your master is back to being a depraved lord again, and I can see he put you up to it." I smirked up at Ivan. "How are you going to make it up to me now, Lord Rothvale?"

He grinned back at me, looking far too handsome for his own good, and owning that too, as well as his prank on me. "Oh, I have a few ideas, Miss Hargreave, but first I need to get off this beast and come down there where you are and give you a kiss."

"Please, my lord."

He hopped down easily from Pontus's great height as if he'd done it a thousand times and stalked forward, reaching me in two long steps.

He loomed over me, our bodies very close but not quite touching, as he stared down at me with an expression I'd come to know and to crave. His lordly look of dominance and control sparking harshly at me from deep within his green, green eyes.

I took in a sharp breath because I'd forgotten to breathe, and my lungs needed a bit of oxygen to keep going. The beauty of him made me forget to breathe.

He reached out a hand and gathered up my hair and pulled it back, exposing my neck as he liked to do and kissed me with all the fervor and lust and possession, he was so expert at doling out. His tongue speared into me deeply, holding me captive as he took his time owning my mouth and exploring unhurriedly with his. Eventually he retreated his tongue to focus on soft bites and nibbles at my lips, and then below my ear at my jaw. I could go back to breathing again, but sadly, he wasn't inside me anymore.

"I missed you," I whispered against the side of his lips, feeling the prick of his beard stubble pressing against my skin, making me shiver just the tiniest bit.

"I do love hearing you say those three words to me." He pulled his lips away enough to look me in the eyes.

"You do?"

"Very much. You're the first person to ever say them to me in this sort of context, and I find hearing the words coming off your pretty lips, Miss Hargreave, to be, quite... something of the marvelous."

I wrapped my arms around him and gave him the hug I wished I could've given him when Mr. Finnegan was telling me the story of his life an hour ago. He pulled me in closer, pressing firm kisses to my head, and we just stayed that way for a bit. Hugging each other in the field with a horse and two greyhounds milling around amongst the wildflowers.

On the Jane Austen novel swoon scale? A solid ten.

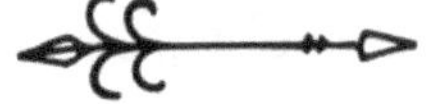

IT WAS SAFE TO SAY that Owen, my sixteen-year-old stable hand, and Marjorie's oldest son, was crushing hard on Gabrielle as he saddled Athena and brought her around to the mounting block where we waited. *Better get used to it, lad. No use fighting your feelings, but just remember she's already taken.* I almost spoke out loud but thought better of it, because I didn't want to mortify the boy for no reason. Young blokes can't help themselves from admiring a beautiful woman. Especially when she looked like Gabrielle in her smart red jacket and bespoke jeans that fit like sin over her mile-long legs I wanted wrapped around my hips—or my face.

Not Owen's fault his cheeks turned dark pink whenever she asked him a question or thanked him.

I took over for helping her mount up and seating her though. Nobody needed to be putting paws on her but me, thank you very much. Still the handsy, depraved bastard as before. Nothing had changed.

With the dogs following the whole way, I led her on a stroll by the coast first, since the day was sunny, we could appreciate the rarely possible view across the sea. "Is that the coast of Scotland I'm seeing?" she asked, pointing.

"From right here on the eastern coast of County Down on a clear day, I can see the Isle of Man. On a sparkling clear day, I can see the Rhinns and the Mull of Galloway in Scotland." I showed her where to look and she nodded her head excitedly as the cliffs of the peninsula came into view for her.

"This is just breathtaking. I realize it doesn't always look like this, nor is the scene always this perfect."

"Quite breathtaking today, I agree." Again, she didn't know I was referring to her and not the view, which was perfection on a normal day, but today the picture-perfect view had some competition. In the form of Gabrielle on Athena with her long hair blowing back in the breeze in tandem with Athena's mane and tail. They shared the same mahogany color, too. A goddess on a mythical steed. A woman who could ride. What more description of perfection was there? I looked forward to doing this with her often, something we could enjoy together when we needed a break.

After we left the coast we headed inland again, and I took her to a place where I figured she might find useful for her research of the paintings. The cemetery where my ancestors were buried beside the willow trees. The dogs beat us to it, knowing my destination probably. They did love the chance to run hell-for-leather at racing speeds.

I dismounted first and then lifted her down from Athena, keeping my hands on her even after I had her safely on the ground. I couldn't help tipping her chin up to meet my lips either. "I need to kiss you again."

"I think you should, Lord Rothvale, it's been a while," she teased.

"Are you being cheeky, Miss Hargreave? Will you require some of my special discipline?"

"Probably, yes, but later when we're not visiting your ancestor's graves."

"Right. Let's go say hello to them, shall we?" I took her hand and led us through the metal gates, creaking as it shut behind us.

She walked right up to the crypt where ROTHVALE was carved into the small marble building that held the earthly remains of two particularly important people who had linked

Gabrielle and I together in a way I could never have imagined.

"Graham and Imogene Everley are buried here in this crypt at Donadea. Lord Rothvale number nine, the man responsible for Tristan Mallerton's career..." She was visibly awed by being here, I could see it clearly in the expression on her beautiful face. "Wow. I'm just so—overwhelmed. I guess the best word to describe being here right now."

"Why overwhelmed, Gabrielle?"

"I don't know how to explain it, really. It's strange, but you have all of this history and amazing connection to this family who did so much for the Romanticism art movement worldwide, and it's my life's work to be studying the paintings of a certain artist who was as close as family could be without being related by blood to your family. If number nine had never mentored Mallerton, then he wouldn't have become a great master, and I wouldn't be studying his work, and you wouldn't have a houseful of his paintings, or ever needed me to come here—"

I kissed her silent, as I often did. It was

effective, so why change something working fine already. When I was good and finished, and not a moment sooner, I pulled back just enough so I could look into her eyes. "I *know*, Gabrielle. And that's why I wanted to bring you here to pay your respects. They were important people to your life's work and your studies, and I thought you might appreciate the chance to actually meet them... in a way. Their spirits are here, and they must have loved Donadea very much to live out the remainder of their lives here rather than at the estate in Warwickshire where it was expected they would. It's the fates hard at work again that make it all so special." I kissed her again and breathed in the scent of her hair before releasing her... reluctantly. I was needy now and couldn't even imagine how I'd be once I dropped her back in London at her flat tomorrow morning. I could only guess it wouldn't go very well on my part. We would be needing a renegotiation of terms ASAP for days spent in London.

"It is special here, Ivan. Thank you for bringing me to meet them. I am truly honored to know your great-great-grandparents. I think they would approve of what you're doing here, very much so. You're saving their legacy of priceless art the whole world should be able to enjoy instead of being forgotten away in a beautiful mansion on the coast of County Down... where it's at great liability being stored unsecured in a private home."

I gave her a head bow. "I know that too, Gabrielle. I cannot secure it in my house—not properly. I know you are correct, and that is why I *need you* here to help me with the art."

I need you here anyway... for me, too.

"Of course. I am going to help you with the art, and we'll figure it out together, I promise."

"Thank you. I know with it now in your very capable hands you'll tell me what's best."

"I found Imogene's journals from the beginning of her marriage up through five years and hope to shed provenance on the creation of some of the paintings in the collection. I'm really looking forward to getting into them." She looked happy about the prospect of reading.

"Gabrielle, if you had to make a valuation on the works you've seen thus far as a whole, could you make a guess—give me a ballpark on what it's worth?"

"Oh boy. I figured you were going to ask me at some point and it's just not as easy as appraising a single work and then tabulating a total. Fine art sales are the last big money investments which are unregulated by government. Paintings may have no ceiling at all, particularly when works come onto the market previously unknown—as is pretty much your entire collection from what I can tell."

"Really? That much of the collection is unknown?"

"I'm afraid so, but there's more, Ivan. I've spotted several possible Dutch Masters like Bruegel, Vermeer, and what looks clearly to be a Van Gogh with the usual 'Vincent' painted on the vase of white camellias maybe? Not to mention at least six, but possibly more unknown Mallertons, just scattered here and there around your house. I haven't even been in all the rooms yet, but now that I understand his relationship with your family, I'm betting there will be more."

"Why am I getting the feeling you're about to drop a bomb on me, Gabrielle?" I had to ask because I could see she was starting to get stressed the more she talked about the art. Her skin was flushed, and she began wringing her hands the longer she spoke.

"Because there *is* a bomb drop, and it could be a *very* big bomb, and it makes me nervous just speaking his name out loud!" she wailed.

"Come here, kitten, let me hold you while you tell me." I drew her against me and leaned up against a tree and waited. "You just start talking when you're ready, and I will listen to every word, okay?"

She nodded against my chest and took a deep breath and just let me hold her for a minute. I could feel her relaxing a little as I rubbed circles on her back and waited for her to begin.

"You have—there is a *Leda and the Swan* painting in the gallery that looks frighteningly authentic—like a... *Michelangelo*. It scared the crap out of me when I first spotted it. There are other Italian works in the collection, so it's not unreasonable to believe Graham was actively collecting Italian pieces from the period. I've been afraid to even speak the name Michelangelo out loud, and you have to understand it could have been collected at any time, and unless I can find some purchase documentation or written records of such an acquisition in Imogene's diaries, I won't be able to tell you if it was done by him. Michelangelo is way above my expertise and knowledge, on a good day. What I do know is that many artists painted *Leda and the Swan,* but a large portion of the Leda paintings were destroyed later by puritanicals who saw them as obscene. Well, some of them are, quite frankly. A woman being fucked by a swan and not all of them show mere suggestions of the sex. Some are very graphic, like really filthy five-hundred-year-old bestiality porn. Michelangelo is known to have painted a Leda, but it's never turned up anywhere and believed to have been destroyed sometime in the eighteenth century. So, if your Leda is an authentic Michelangelo, not only is it valuable for being his work, but valuable by attrition because it survived the calculated destruction of all Leda paintings over the centuries. Your value is in the high hundreds of millions by my best guess. If you have Michelangelo's Leda, then you have a billion plus pounds of art on your hands. There's no knowing how high those paintings will go on the auction block."

I rubbed up and down her back and soaked it all in. It was far more than I'd believed the collection to be worth before she came here, but then that couldn't be such a surprise. I'd been in denial, putting off dealing with the art for the last four years. I'd needed Gabrielle for a very long time before she ever got here. "Thank you for telling me, kitten. I know it's a huge responsibility dropped onto your shoulders, but you're going to do magnificently, and we'll just take it one step at a time, cliché or not, until we know what the best course of action is."

"I understand why you needed the NDA from me. Nobody can know this art is here, Ivan. It's far too valuable for disclosing its existence until it can be moved, or the security *way* upgraded. After the drone incident I think you need to be worried. I'm worried and I just work here."

I couldn't help chuckling at her last comment. "You're far more than someone who *just works here*, Gabrielle. I hope you understand me well on that point."

"I feel... I *am* important to you. I do feel that

from you. I hope you feel it from me too, Ivan, how important you are to me."

I pulled her lips up to mine and I kissed her... and I kissed her... and I kissed her.

I wasn't sure I could ever stop kissing her.

I LOVED IT WHEN he kissed me unexpectedly. I could be speaking and telling him something important and he'd just lay one on me and that would be the end of whatever I was saying. Lord Rothvale was a bit of a romantic, it seemed. I wondered if he would be this way after we spent more time together. Would he still be romantic with me?

When Ivan finally ended the kiss, the sun had slipped behind some ominous clouds, looking quite ready to pour down on us. He quickly led me toward the horses, impatient to get going. "Wind has shifted. We need to start back before the rain comes. I won't have you ill again from being trapped in the cold and wet."

"Good idea, because I do not want to be ill again." As he boosted me up onto Athena and then mounted up onto Pontus, the most powerful force came over me when I sent my silent goodbyes and my love to Graham and Imogene, resting together in their crypt, under peaceful willows swaying quietly in the breeze.

As we rode off with the dogs racing madly alongside the horses, I really did feel as if I had met them in person. That I now knew them, as they now knew me. We'd been formally introduced, and now we could communicate together about what to do with their priceless paintings. I could go to them and ask for advice and maybe somehow, through the ether and the magic of being together in the same space on this small spot on the earth, they might be able to show me what I needed to do. I felt they somehow knew I was here to protect and keep their legacy safe for the world to enjoy for generations to come.

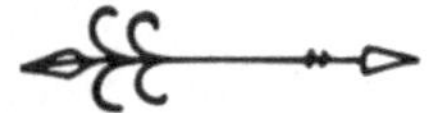

WE NEARLY MADE IT before the rain descended. *Nearly* being the operative word.

The truth? We got good and caught in a summer rainstorm.

As we neared the horse barns, it was drenching down so furiously Ivan shouted over at me, "Just ride her in through the door!"

I didn't have to be told twice. I steered Athena through the open doors and rode her right inside the barn with no problem. As soon as we were under the shelter of the roof, the sound of the pounding rain on the tiles roared like a freight train up over our heads.

Ivan helped me down from Athena and handed her off quickly to Owen along with Pontus. Both horses would have to be rubbed down and then tucked in their stalls with a blanket. "Owen, can you please make sure they both get an extra scoop of oats?" I asked as he started to lead them away.

"Yep. I'll make sure of it, miss," he replied with a nod of his head, his cheeks flushing red.

"Thank you, Owen."

"You've got our young master Owen wrapped around your little finger, I see, Miss Hargreave. Don't you think you should let him know you're taken already? Spare the boy his poor heart from unrequited love?"

"Oh? But... am I taken?"

"You most certainly are." He raised a stern eyebrow at me.

"Hmm. I don't know what you're talking about, Mr. Everley. As usual, you're speaking to me in riddles and mysteries I don't understand at all. If I were *taken,* as you say, then don't you think I'd know his name?" I could tell this was going to be fun.

"You don't know his name?" He stalked toward me slowly, backing me into the nearest empty stall.

I shook my head at him and tried to keep a straight face. "I do not."

"*I* know his name, Miss Hargreave." He

nodded wickedly now that he'd backed me right up against the far wall of the horse stall, where he proceeded to crowd me with his big body until he'd caged me in completely by his arms on either side of my shoulders.

"What is it?" I whispered innocently, completely captivated by the wolf about to pounce on me.

"*My—lord,*" he growled before taking both sides of my face in his hands and holding me very firmly, "is his name."

"I do know him. He makes me feel so special, like a princess, and I don't know why he does it." I brought up my hand and reached out a finger to trace around his lips. "I just know I don't want him to stop."

"He does it because he's fallen in love with you and he's not able to stop."

I smiled and tried to hold back the tears that wanted to spill out of my eyes. "Will it help my lord to know he doesn't ever have to stop, because I've already fallen in love with him?"

He closed his eyes and held them closed for a

moment, looking almost pained but then an expression of relief, and even joy, when he opened them again... to me. "I'll be needing to hear you say that again and again, kitten."

"All right. I'll say it all the time if it helps you to believe it's true." I tucked a piece of his hair around his ear and then did the same to the other side.

"Say it to me now."

"I love you, my lord. *My* Lord Rothvale."

THE END

OF

PART 2

NEXT IN SERIES

The Rothvale Legacy

~ Book III ~

So by now you know we're not done with Ivan and Gabrielle. Not even close. There's so much more coming for these two. I'm hard at work on the third part of the Rothvale Legacy, **Heart & Arrow** so it's safe to say that Ivan and Gabrielle's story will be just as long and eventful as Ethan and Brynne's, so there's much to look forward to for these two passionate lovers. And I'm very happy about that because I'm not ready to say goodbye to my kinky Lord and his art-loving Lady just yet.

xoxo R

ACKNOWLEDGMENTS

I have some heartfelt thanks for keeping me sane and on the writerly path I need to remain on. Seriously, I wouldn't be able to manage if not for two incredibly special people.

Words are insufficient anyway, and I am sure you both know how much I love you. My heart is full to bursting with it.

To my husband and my boys, I thank you for being so supportive of this, my life, and for joining me on the journey.

Thank you to Thom and Helen in London for their brilliant assistance with wordsmithing the Brit terminology and vernacular. You probably have no idea how much I look forward to seeing your notes in my manuscript. It's like opening a much-awaited package. The language of Britain is a thing of magical beauty to me, it always has been, and it always will be.

Quite simply, I am blessed, and I know this from the experiences I have gained in the past year or so. I would be lying if I said it hadn't been a struggle to write this book. Losing both of my parents has been one of the hardest times of my life, and yet I would choose the same path for most of it, if I had to do it all over again. I know more about living now than I did before. Sometimes it takes death to help us understand life to a better degree. I have no regrets, only love...for the two people who created me and formed me as a person. It's always there filling my heart and I know they are both proud of my achievements and share in celebrating with me if from another portal of time and space.

Meeting the people who read and enjoy my books, both in person and online, and making those new connections with them, forging relationships within this business is truly... something of the marvelous.

xxoo R

MR. FINNEGAN'S IRISH SCONES

Yes, it's a real recipe. And yes, it *is* a sacred

experience to eat one!

Image by: **bbcgoodfood.com**

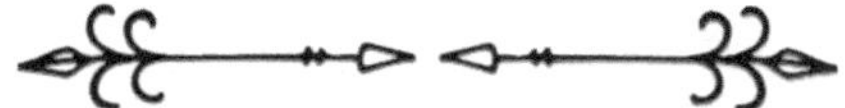

INGREDIENTS

- 3 ½ cups (16oz/497g) all-purpose flour
- 5 teaspoons baking powder, leveled
- 1 generous pinch of salt
- ¼ cup (2oz/60g) sugar
- ½ cup (2½oz/71g) cold, cubed, salted butter
- 1 egg
- ¼ cup (2floz/57ml) double cream
- ¾ cup (6floz/170ml) whole milk
- milk to glaze

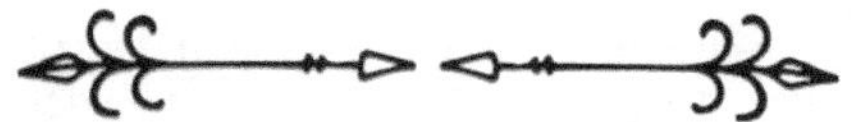

INSTRUCTIONS

1. In a large bowl mix the dry ingredients together.

2. Rub in the cold butter with your fingers until it resembles breadcrumbs.

3. If adding dried fruit or chocolate chips *e.g.* currants, berries, poppy seeds, citrus rind, *etc.* add them now *before* you add in the liquid.

4. Combine beaten egg with milk and cream, then pour into the flour mixture. (you may substitute double cream with heavy cream if you wish)

5. With an open hand, loosely mix together until a dough forms. The bowl should be clean of dough.

6. Turn dough onto a floured work surface.

7. Knead lightly to give the dough a smooth surface.

8. Pat your dough down with your hand until a 1 inch thick circle is formed.

9. With a round cutter (or glass) cut out scones. Makes around 12.

10. Place evenly on baking tray. Then glaze with milk to give scones a golden top when baked.

11. Bake at 350°F (18O°C) for 35 minutes.

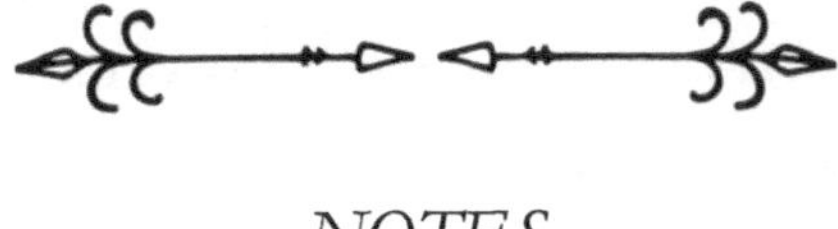

NOTES

Enjoy with Irish butter, jam, and clotted cream. Scones are best eaten the day they are baked but the next day you can pop them back in the oven to freshen them up again.

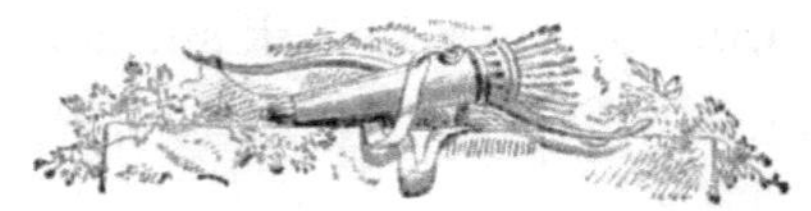

ABOUT THE AUTHOR

Raine has been reading romance novels since she picked up that first Barbara Cartland paperback at the tender age of thirteen. She thinks it was *The Flame is Love* from 1975. And it's a safe bet she'll never stop reading romance novels because now she writes them too. Granted, Raine's stories are edgy enough to turn Ms. Cartland in her grave, but to her way of thinking, a tall, dark and handsome hero never goes out of fashion. Never! Writing sexy romance stories pretty much fills her days now... for which she keeps pinching herself to make sure she's not dreaming. #Truth

Raine has a prince of a husband and two brilliant sons...and two very bouncy but beloved Italian greyhounds to pull her back into the real world if the writing takes her too far away. Her sons know she likes to write stories but have never asked to read any. *Thank. God.* The greyhounds are likely to be in her lap while she writes the stories—both dogs at the same time.

All are welcome to connect with Raine on Facebook in her reader group **@Raine Miller Romance Readers** anytime.

BOOKS BY RAINE MILLER

The ROTHVALE LEGACY

Historical Prequel: The MUSE

PRICELESS, Part 1

My LORD, Part 2

HEART and ARROW, Part 3

BLACKSTONE DYNASTY

FILTHY RICH

FILTHY LIES

The BLACKSTONE AFFAIR

NAKED, Part 1

ALL IN, Part 2

EYES WIDE OPEN, Part 3

RARE and PRECIOUS THINGS, Part 4

CONTEMPORARY ROMANCE

CHERRY GIRL

HUSBAND MATERIAL

LOVELY PINK

NOTES

NOTES

NOTES